lury.gibson was founded in 1999. Their first production to feature
detective Arthur C. Dogg was the acclaimed *Dangerous Data*.
Blood Data is his second investigation.

Acclaim for
DANGEROUS DATA

'Dogg is a new breed of gumshoe and *Dangerous Data* is a new breed of
thriller. It is suitably gripping . . . and it is terrifyingly convincing . . . It is
much more interesting than a straightforward panic attack about the end
of privacy. Dogg is not only a detective, he is also a philosopher of the
information revolution . . . Our society has yet to recognise that "data
protection" is an oxymoron. If this novel helps awaken us to that truth,
then it has to be welcomed. I doubt there will be a more important novel
published this year'
Guardian

'The concept of a data detective is an eye-opener. Credit card transactions,
bar codes, education records, e-mails, store cards, court files, cab accounts
– all generate data. Armed with the right software and a bit of nous you
could find out anything about anyone'
Focus

'*Dangerous Data* is an intriguing collaboration which relies on everyday
details to present its story of two university pals with nice, consumer-viable
lifestyles – the records of which point to a triangle of deceit, subterfuge
and wilfully obscured past transgressions . . . Compelling reading for
conspiracy theorists who might realise this Dogg's bark is all about bytes'
i-D Magazine

'Frighteningly good . . . terrifying, not least because so much of it is
believable'
Arena

'It's petrifying stuff and is enough to scare you off ever sending another
e-mail, doing a web search or making a phone call again'
U Magazine

Blood Data

LURY.GIBSON

CORGI BOOKS

BLOOD DATA
A CORGI BOOK : 0 552 14966 7

Originally published in Great Britain by Bantam Press,
a division of Transworld Publishers

PRINTING HISTORY
Bantam Press edition published 2002
Corgi edition published 2003

1 3 5 7 9 10 8 6 4 2

Copyright © Adam Lury and Simon Gibson 2002

Set in Optima/Zurich by
Falcon Oast Graphic Art Ltd.

Corgi Books are published by Transworld Publishers,
61–63 Uxbridge Road, London W5 5SA,
a division of The Random House Group Ltd,
in Australia by Random House Australia (Pty) Ltd,
20 Alfred Street, Milsons Point, Sydney, NSW 2061, Australia,
in New Zealand by Random House New Zealand Ltd,
18 Poland Road, Glenfield, Auckland 10, New Zealand
and in South Africa by Random House (Pty) Ltd,
Endulini, 5a Jubilee Road, Parktown 2193, South Africa.

Printed and bound in Great Britain by
Cox & Wyman Ltd, Reading, Berkshire.

BLOOD DATA

Standard Life

APPLICATION FOR LIFETIME PROTECTION SERIES

The answers you give to the questions on this form are used to assess the material risk of the insurance contract for which you are applying. The questions are designed to obtain material facts likely to be relevant, for example information about your health.

Failure to disclose all such material facts could make the insurance contract void.

Have you ever had any heart disorder, high blood pressure, stroke, circularity disorder, any form of cancer, diabetes, kidney disorder, numbness, paralysis or multiple sclerosis, arthritis or back trouble, depression or psychiatric disorder?

Have your parents, brothers or sisters had any heart or circulatory disease, stroke, diabetes, kidney disease or cancer before age 60 or any hereditary condition? If you answer 'Yes', give details in the box below of the relative[s] affected, nature of medical condition, age at which it first occurred and current age [or if dead, age at death].

Every time you give data, it's like a little blood sample. A little red tube of you. Your name written on the label. Taken off for analysis. Only with this sample you don't get to see the results. Other people are running the diagnosis: about what you buy, where you go, who you are. Getting to know you, getting to know you right down to your little red corpuscles. Maybe you're not worried about what they discover. Just a trivial bit of data after all: a few shopping trips. Nothing you put any store by. But what if you could see the results and there was something on the printout you didn't recognize? What would you do?

Easy – you'd deny the data. People do it all the time. I call it credit card syndrome. Here's how it goes: you're going through your statement and you come across this item on the list: £30.09 petrol, BP Haringey. And you think to yourself, 'That's not right. I've never been to Haringey.' So you check your diary and there was no mention of a meeting in Haringey that day. And the more you think about it the more convinced you are: you've never been to Haringey. So you just have to call the credit card company. By this stage you're so certain of your facts that the moment you connect with an 'agent', you set off with this whole long story, about how you've never been to Haringey and just before you get to the punchline, where you say, 'so that proves it . . .' just at that point – Christ – the circuit inside your head makes a click. And suddenly you remember that you went to see John Collins last month and the motorway was closed by an accident, so you had to come back another way and you were running short of petrol and so you stopped . . . at a BP garage in Haringey.

And in that moment your mind expands; you realize there's a whole dimension to your life that you choose to filter out. As a matter of course, you edit down your details, make them fit your inner story. But the facts don't lie. As other people can tell you, there's more on your file than you think. They've got the data on you, in that little blood sample.

All of which means that the age-old question 'Who do you think you are?' has a very new twist. For the first time other people can know you better than you know yourself. They can know everything about you. Like when you're going to die.

File date: 03/01/02   12.34 p.m.

H.M. Coroner's Report

<u>**Elizabeth Jane Rowans**</u>

one gold wedding ring on third finger of left hand
small watch on left arm
a three acorn brooch on blouse in front
one small catholic cross under blouse
blue denim trousers and red shoes
tattoo of two hearts with arrow, above the right knee, names Roy on right
side and Josh on the left side
shot wound in left breast going into chest
wound on elbow, fracturing the bone
gunshot wound to bone of first finger, right hand
another to the middle finger, right hand.

<u>**Dogg File:**</u>

Client: Benjamin Franks (adoptive name)
Search Aim: Whereabouts of Real Mother

We die alone, though we don't necessarily mean to. I remember saying that to someone once. They're long gone now.

What interests me about the dead is that their data lives on, even though their file gets closed. Take those innocent questions you get asked on consumer questionnaires. A number of them are about your parents or family. Often deceased. That means some of the data on your file belongs to other people, dead people. Dead data living on.

The dead bequeath their data to you, and sometimes frankly you wish they hadn't. Because the dead's data can sure mess up your file. Play havoc with a life assurance application, or the job you want to get, or the career path you've chosen. Take this case I was working on last week for a young lawyer, Benjamin Franks. He had been adopted and he'd asked me to find his real mother. I tracked her down all right, found she was a convicted criminal. Released from jail, she died in what looked like a gangland shooting. This was not the sort of news that was going to sit well on the lawyer's file. It wasn't going to help his partnership prospects – not one bit – and not surprisingly he told me to bury the file. Pity. It made interesting reading. She must have been quite a girl.

The Dogg
DATA DETECTIVE

Looking for things you didn't know were there.

thedogg@acdogg.co.uk

Me, I am a data detective: Arthur C. Dogg. The Numero Uno in my field. If there is information held on you on a database – no matter where – I can access it. Or maybe I should say, if you know a secret about yourself you don't want shared with others – you'd better start praying I'm not on your case. Because as the great philosopher John Lennon should have said: there's nothing you can know that can't be known.

All of life is digital. Stored on databases: everything from driving offences to medical records. I deal in the knowable. I allow my clients to experience facts, secrets they could not discover in any other way. My goal is to set information free – and earn a living while I'm at it.

I'm a freelance. Work for anyone and everyone. Don't have to worry how my CV reads. In fact, for some clients, the worse it reads the better. People expect their detectives to be a little toasted on the inside.

And life insurance? Kills me, that phrase 'life insurance'; what they mean is death insurance. Well I sure don't worry about that. I am the Dogg and ever more shall be so. They will not know my source code. If they do have a file on me, it just shows I exist. My file is as 'live' as it can get. I am just me. Right here in the now. Looking for things that most people would rather weren't found.

Sometimes, my clients may not like what I discover – in fact I warn them of this in advance. 'Never ask a question you don't want to hear the answer to.' That's what I say. It's the best advice. It's the only advice a detective can give. To a client, or to himself. I should learn to remind myself of that, every time a new job comes in. Even the most innocent of jobs.

04/01/02   15.35

e-mail from giselle@destinyresearch.co.uk

Dear Mr Dogg

I have heard so much about you, I feel like we've met already. Think I have a job that will truly test your powers. Perhaps take you places you'd rather not go. If you're as good as they say you are, you'll love it. If not, you won't come through unscathed. Enticing isn't it.

Let me know if I can count on you – and of course your rates of pay.

best regards
Giselle Jackson

If I had an office it would say Arthur C. Dogg, Data Detective, on the brass plate outside. I would have a bottle of whisky in my top drawer and a handsome Beretta in the bottom. My long-suffering but curvaceous secretary would screen my calls and occasionally disturb my reverie with a knock at the door and a whispered: 'Mr Dogg there's a lady to see you. She seems quite insistent.'

Sad to say the data detective has none of the above, though I confess to a weakness for mysterious and insistent lady callers. A weakness is a good thing in a man, it opens up his fate. And fate is especially intriguing when it comes in smelling of Chanel, the way this Giselle did.

Full of brash and bravado, like she wants to take me on. Well I'm up for the game. As long as there's money on the table.

04/01/02   15.37

Dear Ms Jackson

Thank you for your enquiry. If you forward the details of the individuals you wish me to observe, I shall take the matter from there.

Surveillance fees are as follows: £500 for location of the individual and £200 per week subsequently.

I can begin the case as soon as I receive the details.

Yours
Arthur C Dogg

Dear Dogg

So formal, Dogg. Just call me Giselle. I don't bite, you know.

Your first subject is Gerald John Keatring. Address: 27 Mountjoy Court London E17 4LJ.

Relax. Loosen up. Enjoy the ride.
Giselle

OK I'm weak. I take the job. Detection is my life. It's what I do; all I can do. Indeed the Dogg has often wondered: do you become what you do, or do what you are? Conventional wisdom says a bit of both. But then conventional wisdom always likes a compromise.

All that matters right now is that I enjoy my job. I'm paid to follow patterns in the data trail. This isn't always as simple as it sounds. It's not a nice, straight line job. In fact, if you're going to be a detective, the first thing you have to understand is that data is not linear. When you're searching through a database there's no difference between forwards, or sideways or back. It's all in the same dimension. All in the same time frame – what I like to call 'the data present'. So the clues you're looking for can come from anywhere. What might appear to the untrained eye as a digression is actually right on the scent. The secret is to let go. Treat every detail and fact as equally important. Look for the patterns that link them together.

I never let up, not for one moment. I'm there whenever my subjects move in the material world. It's like I have them under constant surveillance, yet the only screen I'm looking at is my own.

Imagine if twenty-four hours a day, someone had a video camera on you. That would be an objective record of your day. But would you recognize yourself in this digital mirror? Would you like what you saw?

How about Gerald John Keatring? How's he going to like what I make of him in action replay? Life's getting like that red button on the TV screen. The red one you can press to select a player to follow through a football game. Interactive TV. You are the players. The Dogg is the producer. How do you like my show?

05/01/02

<u>Gerald John Keatring File</u>

Gerald John Keatring
b. Brentwood, Essex 24/8/66
Nat. Ins. No.   TN 8720864J
Nat. Health No.   736442165
Status   Registered Unemployed

Address   27 Mountjoy Court E17 4LJ
Telephone   020 8985 8597
Mobile   077371329873

Address assigned to Patricia Helen Sampson
b. London 31/3/62
Nat. Ins. No.   TQ 7432216P
Nat. Health No.   872119631
Status   Council tenant

Tenancy commenced 1/8/95

Bank Acct   NatWest
details pending . . .
Occupation   Store Clerk Tesco Supermarkets

Two children
Kevin Thomas Sampson b. 17/3/94, father unknown
Daniel John Sampson b. 23/6/95, father registered as Gerald John Keatring

See, it doesn't take long for the information to start coming through, for the profile to emerge. Gerald lives with his girlfriend. They have a modest abode in East London.

She definitely has a past. She's not unfamiliar with the fifty ways to leave her lover exactly. There are two sons from different fathers. Growing up in the same house. Both growing up with Gerald. How does that affect a child, growing up within a family where dad isn't dad? The Dogg does not know how this feels, but knows it would feel different; leave its mark.

Not a lot of money floating around 27 Mountjoy Court, I'd guess. What little there is will be spent in cash. Which doesn't make it easy for the Dogg to follow his prey. But there's one big positive. Gerald has a mobile phone.

The mobile. Symbol of freedom and flexibility, but actually she's a transvestite bitch. When she first hit the streets, the mobile was locked in the wrong body: all macho, big and beefy. Now she's had the op. She's feminine. She's gone petite, but more than that she's gone all celebratory yet discreet. She's a paradox, a chameleon, a siren with different wardrobes and different songs. There's no escaping her call, no matter how you cover your ears.

Of course for the data detective the mobile is often far more useful than simply a means of calling the office for messages. In fact the mobile has caused a revolution, because the mobile phone is your perfect personal tagging device. Everyone's tagged without knowing it – and they pay for the line rental! The reason is that thanks to the satellites up there in the stars a call can be traced to within ten metres. I can know not only who you called, but where you called from, twenty-four hours a day.

05/01/02   02.42

Gerald John Keatring File

Orange PCS
Historical Call Records w/c 31/12/01

Cell IDS
Cell Data CA

Start	End	Number Calling	Start Time/Date
21693	21693	07737 1329873	11.58.06
38204	38204	07737 1329873	13.14.21
37269	37269	07737 1329873	14.24.35
37269	37269	07737 1329873	14.27.41
37269	37269	07737 1329873	14.38.09
25611	25611	07737 1329873	16.59.12

Data Protection Act

An individual is entitled to have communicated to him in an intelligible form the information constituting any personal data of which that individual is the data subject.

www.geocaching.com

Geocaching was conceived last year, after the US Defense Department stopped scrambling signals sent from orbiting satellites to GPS devices. That increased their accuracy from about 100 metres to roughly four, making it possible to pinpoint very specific locations.

Gerald. Can you hear me, Gerald? No? OK, I'm only teasing. But I am inside your mobile handset, with you every step of the day. And Gerald, you're not doing much to make a better life for yourself are you? Judging from your call pattern, most of your days are spent in the bookmakers and most of your evenings in the pub.

The lure of the bookmaker. The Dogg admits to being a gambler, though more of a casino man. Bookmakers are rather less glamorous: windowless rooms, cigarette stubs on the floor, the girl behind the counter with a scar high on her neck behind her ear, the young guy who wants to be a jockey wearing a track suit like he's been out training, a couple of Polish heavies who work on the local building site, a black guy with a rasta hat and loud, forced laugh, the woman with the fake Vuitton shoulder bag. Copies of the *Racing Post* pinned to the walls: the punter's horoscope. A large white board at the end of the room, with printed lists of the names of the runners and prices marked against them in red felt pen. This is a place that offers the chance to win, but only for born losers.

I'd say Gerald likes the fellowship of gambling; talking with your mates, always on about the bets that so nearly came off. Gambling is hope and hope is companionship.

Because the guy on the tannoy system is still calling the horses: 'They're under starter's orders at Hexham . . . 5–4 the field at Windsor . . . They're off at Hexham.' And the voice is like fate or blind justice or even death, just calling like it is. No emotion at the wheel of chance he's calling. The heartless voice of a commentator who's seen everything, every hard luck story: 'They are all just punters to me.'

Oh yes, Dogg can understand the lure of an afternoon in hope. So he sympathizes with Gerald. But that doesn't stop the Dogg from wondering where Gerald is getting the money from to booze and bet – when you're only receiving £45 a week on unemployment benefit. (Maybe he's nicking it off his girlfriend.) Gerald's also making quite a few calls from these safe havens. Rather more than I would expect if they were simply social calls. A final observation: one call doesn't fit the pattern. From a factory unit. Maybe you went for a job interview, Gerald.

Gerald John Keatring File

Orange PCS
Historical Call Records w/c 07/01/02

Cell IDS Cell Data CA

Start	End	Number Calling	Start Time/Date
43692	43692	07737 1329873	20.58.06
39320	39320	07737 1329873	21.17.31
33557	33557	07737 1329873	21.34.24
33357	33357	07737 1329873	22.45.23
38279	38279	07737 1329873	23.12.38

www.stripinfo.co.uk/main/pub

Strip Info >> Pub List

Traders	222 Shoreditch High Street
Rainbow Sports Bar	
The White Horse	64 Shoreditch High Street
Crown & Shuttle	223 Shoreditch High Street
Lord Nelson	17 Mora Street
Nag's Head	17/19 Whitechapel Road
Griffin	125 Clerkenwell Road
Metropolis	234 Cambridge Heath Road
The Spread Eagle	1–3 Kingsland Road
Brown's	1 Hackney Road
Ye Olde Axe	69 Hackney Road
Commercial Tavern	Commercial Street
The Norfolk Village	220 Shoreditch High Street
Ten Bells	84 Commercial Street
Seven Stars	49 Brick Lane
Flying Scotsman	4 Caledonian Road

www.fleshcity.org/STRIP/VENUES

THE SPREAD EAGLE

The Venue
Located just over the road from Brown's, this strip-pub undergoes a precarious existence. The last (temporary) closure was due to the minor technicality of operating without the required licence.

Decided I needed an evening out and given the circumstances who better for me to spend it with than Gerald? I can follow him round thanks to his log of mobile calls backed up by a Net search on the pubs he visits. In fact we spend quite a riotous time together. In the company of girls.

We start the evening off at the Spread Eagle. An old favourite of Gerald's judging by his mobile data. The pub is a strip legend. Walk in through the entrance door, and the first thing you'll notice is the pool table, right in the centre. The place has recently undergone limited decoration, so it's ramshackle rather than dilapidated. A carpet covers the majority of the bare floorboards. Some of the walls have been half repainted.

The two-foot-high stage is small, about 12' by 6', and this is where all the action takes place. There's a single chrome pole – a token acknowledgement to the modern art of striptease. Good view from the front, though restricted if the people standing ahead of you are taller than you are. If you like things 'up close and personal', then you can stand within two–three foot of the stage. The girls sit a little to the right of the stage, in an area screened off by a low partition. Not many dancers, but it's cosy if you know what I mean. The girls pay a fee to dance here and earn their cash by passing a jug around. They can also supplement their 'jug' money with private dances. The Dogg is in his element.

We then move on to the Metropolis, walking in past a bunch of well turned-out bouncers. A circular stage in the middle of the joint. A couple of pillars restrict visibility and combined with the strobe lighting and copious use of the dry ice machine, viewing's a bit patchy. But the atmos' is like an express train, 'a locomotive hammering through your libido'. One attractive girl gets off stage and is immediately replaced by a more stunning colleague. Quality is the best on the circuit. Each girl starts with a topless routine and then moves on to the full routine, after circulating a pint jug. It takes ten minutes for the jug to go round, such is our appreciation. Go to a booth for a private dancer. Five minutes thunder by, locomotive fashion. Like the guy says, 'She's the psychosexual equivalent of crack cocaine: you want MORE and you want it NOW.'

We round the evening off at Brown's, more jugs, more private dancers. The Dogg determines to get out more often.

Gerald John Keatring File

H.M. Prisons Records

Prisoner No.	DG5684
Gerald John Keatring	
White: British	
Released	29/11/01
Conviction	Robbery
Plea	Guilty
Sentence	4 years, served 43 months, commenced 02/04/98
Prison	Pentonville (remand); Belmarsh (CAT A prison); Latchmere House (CAT C/D)
Previous convictions	Burglary
Custodial sentences	1981–1983
	1988–1991
served three years	
Probation Officer	Mr J. S. Stoffel

www.hmprisonservice.gov.uk/life

Your security category: This makes a difference to where you will serve your sentence and how much freedom you will be allowed in prison. There are four security categories for adults: A, B, C and D.

Category A applies to prisoners who escape or who would be highly dangerous to the public, or the police, or the security of the State, no matter how unlikely that escape might be; and for whom the aim must be to make escape impossible.

Category B applies to prisoners for whom the very highest conditions of security are not necessary, but for whom escape must be made very difficult.

Category C applies to prisoners who cannot be trusted in open conditions, but who do not have the resources and will to make a determined escape attempt.

Category D applies to prisoners who can reasonably be trusted in open conditions.

Know what, those calls that Gerald's making, they're not to his pen pals. And that call he made from a factory unit, it wasn't for a job interview. There were other reasons.

All that time in the pub, putting money in the jugs, yet with no discernible source of income, got me thinking about Gerald. Decided I'd go back into his past a little. And there, straight at the top of the file: his criminal record. Repeated convictions for robbery. Gerald looks like he's the hard man in the crew on a couple of these incidents. If things go wrong, he'll fix them.

Going back into Gerald's past – there's a notion for you. That you can get into someone's past, like it's a real place that you could mark on a map. To me the past is 3D. A space which you can enter like you'd walk into a room, look around and tell exactly what sort of person lives there. Take a glance at the photos on the wall, the loved one, look around the trophy cabinet, the invitations to old parties, the furniture inherited, the scuffs on the carpet. It's all a 3D story shaped by facts.

In Gerald's case there are some bad facts in this back room. Gerald's space is dark lit: naked light bulb, cosh on a table. Money in the drawer. You can tell from this room that Gerald is a professional. He moves from one 'job' to the next; gambling he won't get caught. Enjoying the scene; there are guys who do.

Why didn't Giselle come clean about Gerald's criminal past? If I have learnt anything as a detective, it's how to listen to the spaces; it's what people don't tell you that matters most. That's where you'll find motive. To me this particular gap says that Giselle wants to know about Gerald precisely because of his criminal record.

PATRICIA SAMPSON BANK DETAILS

Branch Address 300 Romford Road, London E7
Account number 284769038
Current balance £154.90
Maximum balance last year £896.76

09/01/02 11.54

Gerald John Keatring File

Gerald John Keatring

Bank Account   Co-operative Current A/C   £3.20
                      581290   72411963
Car purchase 20.12.01
Roger Stern Motors E17
Registration number P242 XFX
Purchase price £2600
Insurance Direct Line Third Party only policy number 23/33728Y56
Policy commenced 21/12/01

TVLA RECORDS

TV Purchase
Dixons, 88 Oxford Street, London W1N 1BX
Hitachi 24" Nicam Stereo Widescreen TV (C24W43ON)   £399.99
JVC Super VHS Video Recorder (HR 56855K)   £199.99

www.botspot.com

In short: **a bot** is a software tool for digging through data. You give a bot directions and it brings back answers. The word is short for robot of course.

On the Web, robots have taken on a new form of life. Since all Web servers are
connected, robot-like software is the perfect way to perform the methodical
searches needed to find information. The term bot has become interchangeable
with **agent**, to indicate that the software can be sent out on a mission, usually to
find information and report back.

OK, we're getting the picture now. Gerald is spending. He's not just blowing a few quid on girls, beer and horses, he's getting big cash from somewhere. New car, TV and video. All paid for in ready money.

How do I know? Well, one of the tricks I have learnt over the years is to keep a watch bot running at the entrance to all government database sites. Among my favourites are those that deal with the absurdly quaint notion of a licence. (I mean come on, guys, we are living in a licence-free world. We can do anything we like, without having to ask you for permission and you insist on this petty tax-raising stunt of a licence. Just call it a tax, and let us get on with our lives will you.) Anyway, however old-fashioned, licences are useful to Dogg: vehicle licences, driving licences, and of course television licences.

Not that Gerald has a television licence. But he should have. We know that because the shop where he bought the TV and video sent a message to the TVLA, giving Gerald's name and address.

Buying in cash didn't save Gerald. The same for that motor he bought. Nothing expensive, I know, but it still shows up on my screen. By such little items, the state – and therefore Dogg – can keep a watch on you. Just out of neighbourly interest of course.

A new car, TV and video. Gerald is living beyond his means. Which of course tells us he's living on someone else's. Gerald is the sort of man who wants more from life, but isn't prepared to wait for it. He wants it now. Wants change now. Probably thinks that if only things had been just a little different he would have run a restaurant instead. And if he could make just a few quid clear, he'd be able to set himself up in something. Only we know from the pattern, that's not what's going to happen to Gerald.

www.innertalk.com/Process_of_Change.html

Most people would like to change something about their lives. For some, it's getting a better job, or losing weight, or improving memory, or accelerating learning abilities, or adding charisma to their personalities and so forth.

The agency of change is within us. It is not a 'thing'. For someone to become prosperous they must think in a different order of magnitude than one who is content with just getting by.

True change is never effortless! We believe that our technology provides for a process of change that has never been easier, but at that, you must be committed for change to occur.

www.VocationLab.com

CHANGE CAREERS – CHANGE YOUR LIFE! FIND YOUR TRUE CALLING

What do you want to do with the rest of your life? Listen to your inner voice and discover your potential. Find your true calling and live it. Your journey starts here . . .

www.gloriousnoise.com

GLORIOUS NOISE – ROCK AND ROLL CAN CHANGE YOUR LIFE

www.proust.com

HOW PROUST CAN CHANGE YOUR LIFE, NOT A NOVEL

www.ivillage.com/fengshui

CHANGE YOUR LIFE WITH FENG SHUI

What part of my life would I like to change?

This is the easy part: Just click on the area you need help with below . . .

Could Gerald's pattern change? Could he go straight, break the habits of a lifetime? It's possible, anything is possible. We have to believe that people can change, don't we?

The basis of life, order, and society of all kinds is hope. We keep criminals and carpenters from going stir crazy by giving them hope. It's the number one opiate.

These days there are whole huge industries peddling hope. It's all they bring to market. And this invisible, intangible stuff sells by the bucket load, by the container load. It outsells everything. Especially the hope of change.

Take self-help books. People buy millions of them but nothing ever changes. The fix they're looking for is imagining change, and that's enough. No need to do anything about it – because if you did do something and you were unsuccessful, you'd have nothing to fall back on; no dreams to comfort you.

And even if you do change, all that's going to matter to other people is your original sin. The truly interesting thing about the reformed alcoholic is that he was an alcoholic. The Weight Watcher of the Year is only remarkable when you see the picture of her as she was (yes, just four months ago!).

So do people really change? Even if they break through the demons of indifference and indolence, even if they summon the supreme effort of will to make that change – aren't they still trapped?

Is that deep down why most of us don't bother? Not because we're afraid of failure. But because we know we can't change. We're cakes baked, not a mixture waiting for the oven.

20/01/02

Gerald John Keatring File

Orange PCS
Historical Call Records w/c 31/12/01

Cell IDS
Cell Data CA

Start	End	Number Calling	Start Time/Date
44693	44693	07737 1329873	21.56.45
44693	44693	07737 1329873	21.58.34
23356	23356	07737 1329873	23.45.45

www.localpub.com

St George and Dragon
297 Stratford High Street

Local for the hard guys of the National Front variety; reportedly gambling in the
back room.

Another evening on the tiles with Gerald. And after our last little out-ing I was rather looking forward to meeting up with the girls again.

But Gerald's got other ideas. Doesn't go to the strip-pubs, instead he heads off to another boozer off his usual beat.

The St George and Dragon. A hard pub on the High Street, Stratford. Gambling joint. Probably walk in to the sound of 70s music. The pop rock era in full swing. Steve Harley and Cockney Rebel: 'Come Up and See Me, Make Me Smile.'

We know Gerald's a bit of a gambler so the Dogg suspects he goes through to the back room.

Gerald John Keatring File

Police National Crime Files
CAD (Computer Aided Dispatch) Report

RECORDED IN IR BY DL007241 AT 20.45 SERIAL 104632

REC BY: DL:IR
PHONE
LOCATION: ST GEORGE AND DRAGON, 297 STRATFORD HIGH ST
TYPE: 05/24
GRADE: 2
ASSIGN: W2, WY1

TIME	USER ID	REMARKS
20.45	182934664	FIGHT IN PROGRESS
		TWO MEN, LOCAL FIRST AID
20.51	182934664	RQST AMBULANCE
		PLS.

This is not the evening entertainment that either Gerald or the Dogg anticipated. The cops are on their way. Some kind of fight has broken out. What was it that Machiavelli said: 'You can't choose whether or not to have a fight, but you can choose when.'

Well this is both good and bad timing, Gerald. Bad because you're in the boozer at the time of the argument, who knows you may be involved, but good because the Dogg is live with the police computer. So we should get to find out what's going on right away.

Gerald John Keatring File

Police National Crime Files
CAD 104632 refers PC 00182 AC ARBUTHNOT takes report at location
AC STN OFFICE

Anonymous call to attend a disturbance at the ST GEORGE public house at 20.45 hours. On arrival 182 AC was shown through a large outdoor room where there were clear signs of a struggle having taken place.

Large amount of blood on the floor. A terrier dog had apparently been injured in the scuffle. The dog was not available for inspection.

Two men were also injured, Gerald John KEATRING, Frank Arthur HARRIS. The former had deep cuts to his left arm, while Mr Harris had suffered slashing to his face, as though he had been cut with a broken bottle. Both were treated with first aid at the scene and an ambulance was subsequently called.

Neither of the two men wish to make any charges against the other. Landlord had no intention of pursuing claim.

It's always difficult in a bar-room fight to know exactly who started things. A comment gets taken the wrong way, some pushing and shoving and pretty soon there's fighting on the tables.

In this case the Dogg has to do some work on the situation. A few clues to go on. The St George is a known gambling joint. The incident took place not in the main bar but an outside room, and a terrier dog was injured in the scuffle. More significantly, the dog wasn't available for inspection.

Something about this sequence doesn't ring true. There's no apparent motive for the fight. And the dog is not around yet the two men are. I'd say the police officer had his suspicions as to what was going on. They weren't gambling with cards. They were gambling on the outcome of a dog fight. Explains why the call to the police was anonymous and why the animal wasn't around – to give a statement. The injuries would have shown that they'd been sustained as a result of bites from another dog. In fact the blood on the floor wasn't just from one dog but two.

Nasty business, dog fighting. Fights can take over an hour and often end in a dog being killed outright. Or maybe one of the dogs will surrender, rolling over and offering its throat or belly to its opponent. Strange language used to describe the fight too: a bite is called 'mouthing'. Nice euphemism. Worst of all, stolen pets – dogs and cats – are often used as suckers, sparring partners and general fodder for upcoming champs to practise on.

My guess of the situation is that Gerald doesn't like the outcome of a fight, or maybe goes to collect and doesn't get paid. Either way another, human, fight begins. With just as much violence, and Gerald doesn't back away. All those days behind bars would have taught you how to handle yourself, Gerald, or maybe you're a natural? A natural. Yeah, it's beginning to look that way, Gerald. A natural scrapper. Always getting into scrapes. Some people are that way; just violent, got nasty tempers and looks like you're one of them, Gerald. 'Violence breeds violence.' That's what they say in the ghettos from Bogota to LA. It just becomes a way of life. A basic pattern that you live by because there's no other pattern on offer.

BURGLARIES OF DOMESTIC DWELLINGS BY TIME OF DAY – ENGLAND AND WALES

Morning	8%
Morning/afternoon	10%
Afternoon	21%
Evening	32%
Evening/night	6%
Night	23%

Home Office

Gerald John Keatring

Prison Medical File

Height	188 cm
Weight	86.4 kg
Blood group	AB
HIV	Negative
Exercise regime	M

If I told you that Gerald got up late, would that surprise you? No, I guess not. You're already building a picture of Gerald from the facts I've given you. You know guys like Gerald don't stir early. They go to work rather later.

I reckoned my client Giselle knows as much about Gerald's 'employment' as I do. But anyway I sent her a report describing his pattern of movements, spending most of the day in betting shops and pubs, high mobile phone usage, no apparent source of income, yet regular spending including some larger ticket items, and last but far from least, his recent fight at the St George. My conclusion: Gerald was back on the job.

21/01/02

e-mail from giselle@destinyresearch.co.uk

Dear Dogg

Great work on Gerald. Can you give me any more on the fight? If so, good; otherwise I'd like you to pick up a new trail. Stanley Rhodes. He'll test your powers – beyond the reach of police observations.

Will pay the same fee as before. OK?

Good luck with this one.
Giselle

Luck is not something the Dogg needs. The Dogg does not trust to luck. I am the consummate professional. My antennae quiver to the least vibration. Right now, I am beginning to sense you're challenging me, Ms Giselle Jackson. 'Beyond the reach of police observations'! Since when did I stop at the stuff that the Boys from the Met pick up? I work with data they've never even thought of. I am the Dogg, remember.

You know those words of Nietzsche's 'Will a self to become a self'? Well, Friedrich, I'm with you, babe. I made myself into the best, I used every ounce of will that a man can get hold of. I invented will. I made my self. I don't need anybody else to help me.

I am the lone Dogg.

Not going to waste my time running a blind trace on Stanley Rhodes. I'm going to go straight to the file, before I start monitoring him.

21/01/02

<u>Stanley Rhodes File</u>

Stanley Rhodes
b. 23.4.64 Manchester
Nat. Ins. No.   TS 74359614X
Nat. Health No.   448263512
Last Address
26 Bantam Gardens SW13 4XT

H.M. Prisons Records

Prisoner No.	FD6129
Stanley Rhodes	
White: British	
Released	14/01/02 (on recommendation of parole board)
Conviction	Possession of a controlled substance Class A
	Trafficking in controlled substance Class A
Plea	Guilty
Sentence	4 Years, served 39 months
Prisons	Pentonville (remand); Brixton (CAT B); Standford Hill (CAT D)
Pre. Convictions	None
Probation Officer	Ms N. Silvers

Have to say I don't like working on drugs files. Too often the whole thing gets messy. You can see it will end in tragedy, but there is no catharsis.

Maybe there never was catharsis. Just an excuse that the Greeks came up with so that they could watch really bad stuff happen on stage. And the scholars agreed with them, called the justification catharsis, a sort of sauna for the soul: sweat it out beside the dramatic coals and then take a cold plunge. If the shock doesn't kill, it'll make you feel terrific. Of course Sigmund, dear Sigmund, Freud went even further; said that aggression was a natural instinct which only intensified if it was not released, either by action or watching violent acts.

To Dogg this is overdoing it. I mean why not just come clean and say that public executions make good theatre? Always have. If they made a TV programme, 'Final Moments – Live from Death Row', millions and millions would watch it. In other words there is within the human frame that which desires to see others suffer. And the desire is not noble, but natural. There is something in suffering we trust.

There's something in punishment we also feel gratified by. Punishment and justice are not the same thing, not associated. Though, as they say, they flourish in the same hedgerow. Justice does not require punishment. Our emotions do. Justice is theory, punishment practice.

Where is the justice in locking up drug pushers like Stanley? I mean I can see the social need, but why call it justice? Bet that's what Stanley Rhodes thought too, when they put him in the slammer. Wonder if Stanley's 'nick' name was 'Scholar' or 'Cecil'?

Well at least I know what sort of subject I'm dealing with now and why – Giselle is studying ex-cons.

20/06/01

Parole Board Report

Stanley Rhodes

'No evidence of drug abuse or of further trading within the prison.
Worked in prison canteen, cleaner in prison chapel. Exemplary
discipline record, co-operated with prison counsellors on strategy after
leaving prison.'

Social Trends 2000

'77% of young male offenders are reconvicted within two years.'

Our new subject seems to have been a model prisoner. Working as a cleaner in the prison chapel – how much more model can you get? Perhaps they called him 'Sweeper' Rhodes.

Obviously, we're not talking big league criminal here. Stanley looks like a guy who got caught and just wanted to get out of there as soon as possible. But equally now that he's out chances are he'll have gone back to his old ways. His old pattern of behaviour will reassert. He'll go back to moving in and out of money, pushing drugs in bars and alleys, at stations and knocking shops.

Of course there are some who'd argue that we should never let people out of prison in the first place. If nearly 80 per cent of young people reoffend, perhaps 80 per cent of all prisoners eligible for release should simply be kept in jail. 'Sorry, lads,' they'd say, 'I know we said we'd let you out. But what's the point? You'll only be back here in a few months and in the interim other innocent people will suffer, so we're just going to keep you in.'

And of course they'd say that this logic needn't just apply to those in prison. If we know that 20 or 30 per cent of a particular community are going to commit a crime, why not round them up before they do? Why wait for the crime?

Shocking, isn't it.

Stanley Rhodes File

14 Belfrew Road
London E1 4XL

Status   Tenant   14/01/02

DVLA   M344 MYL
Registered Driver

Mobile phone   no records
Bank Acct   National Westminster Current A/C
                   30-12-84 46721143
Acct Balance   £210.41
Standing Order   £25.00   Church of Living Saints
                   17/01/02

HALES TAXIS
Licensed Minicabs

140 Fontaine Road
London SW7 6PD
020 8675 8545

Driver Roster
Barnie Coombs
Ralph Hodges
Terry Franklin
Jaz Sugram
Tariq Sugram
Stanley Rhodes

Roster Details
Stanley Rhodes
2200 – 0700 Monday – Saturday

It's late – after 10.30. People are coming out of the theatres around the Haymarket. It's raining. The Dogg is watching on a webcam as theatre goers take their first steps out into the night. He can feel the scene: you've just been entertained by Mr Lloyd Webber. You come out of the hall, humming one of those 'catchy' songs and outside it's pouring down. Not a chance of getting a taxi. You start to walk towards St James's, irritated, still humming one of those songs, and then out of the night a Samaritan comes. He calls, 'Need a cab?' You hesitate. It's raining. You get in. You know you've done wrong. The mini-cab smells of piss and hair lacquer. The combination is revolting yet strangely attractive, like one of those songs. The seats feel furry, but they're made of plastic. Can you last until you get home? Can you bear that music in your head: 'Don't cry for me . . .'

As the Dogg watches on through the webcam, he wonders whether Stanley Rhodes is driving one of the mini-cabs that circle theatreland tonight. Yes – Stanley has gone legitimate. Got a job with a mini-cab firm and doing all right.

No huge spends of cash, so it seems that he's not pushing drugs. Not right now at least. Though of course mini-cab driving would be a perfect cover. But until I get some other signs of 'nocturnal activity' I'm just going to have to rely on the usual markers: sudden spending and lots of calls on the mobile. For the moment at least, Stanley is doing neither.

One more interesting little titbit: Stanley has joined up with the Church of Living Saints. He's been born again. Must have been all that time he spent cleaning the prison chapel. Looks like he's turned the corner – and found the Lord.

Hallelujah.

26/01/02

HALES TAXIS
Licensed Minicabs

Driver Log:	S Rhodes
Driver No.	78

Log Record	2200 to 0700
	25/01 – 26/01

North End Road	Putney High St
Putney High St	Wandsworth Bridge Rd
Kings Rd	Pembridge Villas
Bayswater Rd	Oxford Street
Tottenham Ct Rd	Blackheath
Clerkenwell Rd	Holland Park
Ladbroke Grove	LHR
LHR	Basil Street

Checking out Stanley's driving logs for the past few weeks and frankly they make rather uninspiring reading. The guy works six nights a week, from 10 until 7 the next morning. No skiving that I can see and no obvious patterns. Doesn't look like he's using the mini-cab business for any of his own drops. In fact, if I had to give an opinion right now I'd say he was free from drugs.

The guy does nothing but work and go to church – well church is an approximation in this case. The Church of Living Saints is not exactly mainstream Anglican. But then I guess they'd say there is no mainstream Anglican church any more. The only place that belief still burns is in the fringe sects – like the way it did when Christianity was born. In the catacombs. Christianity is an underground movement, meeting at the sign of the fish, discussing dangerous notions like we're all born equal.

Anyway, Stanley's belief is about the only thing I have on him. Otherwise, there's nothing. No data. No heartbeat. The guy's a flat-liner: when you stop generating data you're more unalive than the dead. At least the dead's files keep running, getting passed on. But with this Stanley, there's silence on the screen. He sits at home, then goes to work, then goes back home. Maybe he's reading. A better guess is that he's meditating. That's what he's learnt inside.

Now I admit that a flatliner like Stanley is rare and therefore worth watching with interest, as an unusual specimen. But he doesn't necessarily read well in my client reports. Could look like I haven't been doing the job properly. I need to get inside that cab with him, check exactly what's going on.

26/01/02   22.56

H A L E S   T A X I S
Licensed Minicabs

Radio Frequency

Base   166MHz
Cab   172MHz

Have tuned in to Stanley's mini-cab frequency and spent the last few hours listening to life on the airways. It's an unusual experience for Dogg. I don't normally get into this kind of data. It's neither pure fact nor fantasy. Half of it is still nice clean data, but it's also mixed up with other human life stuff. The facts about where people are being picked up and dropped off are getting mixed up with who's doing what to whom. I hear the jokes in the background, the actual tones of voice.

This is a netherworld for the Dogg. The field of blurred data. Pure facts confused by noise of life. The facts are there, but they're modified by feelings. And then you're into all sorts of weirdo territory, where everything is touchy-feely. Where the only truth is the mish-mash of soft warm feelings, which offers no truth at all. Only a comfort blanket.

HALES TAXIS
Licensed Minicabs

Driver 78
Set down in Barking. Request closure for the night. Over.

Controller
What's the matter, Stanley? You never ask for a sick note. Not in love are you? Over.

Driver 78
No. Just had a bad lift. Over.

Controller
Anything you want to share with Big Daddy? Over.

Driver 78
Not really. The bad lift started calling me names. Asked why I had a crucifix in the front of my cab. And a picture of Jesus. Over.

Controller
There are a lot of unbelievers out there, Stanley. That's no reason to check out. Over.

Driver 78
Lift also refused to pay. Had to deal with situation manually. Over.

Controller
Any damage? Over.

Driver 78
Driver OK. Lift will need repair. More than just a paint job. Damage to body-work. Leaking when last seen. Over.

Controller
OK, Stanley. Sounds like you had a bad trip. Ride off into morning and vaya con dios amigo. Over.

Listening to Stanley for several nights. Nothing of any note and then at last an incident. He gets physical with one of his clients. Get the feeling Stanley didn't like the client making jibes about his religion. That's not a kind thing to do at one-thirty in the morning. But to not pay your bill – well that's downright mean-spirited. So Stanley sorts him out. By the sound of things he left him cut and bleeding.

OK, Dogg, go on. Ask yourself, 'What did Stanley *feel* about all this?' Was he filled with remorse? Or did Stanley enjoy it? The Dogg would have to say there was something in his tone of voice which said he did. Just a little hint of pleasure.

You see what happens, Dogg! You leave the world of pure data and right away you get tangled up. You get all caught up in whether Stanley got a kick out of head-butting a troublesome punter; feeling his forehead crunch through the narrow bone and tissue of the nose; blood spreading down across his upper lip. The Dogg cannot know what Stanley felt at this time. No more than anyone else can. So although the trickery of listening in on Stanley's cab line gives me a fact that might otherwise have gone undetected, it also raises questions of emotion and motive: did he head-butt the punter because of the money or because of the jibes about religion?

Stick to the objective incident. Watch out for the inner story creeping in. Keep your distance, Dogg. This guy isn't doing you any good.

Stanley Rhodes File

Prison Medical File

Height	190cm
Weight	110 kg on admission
	99.5 kg on release
Blood Group	O
HIV	Negative
Exercise Regime	M

www.ibiblio.org/wm/paint/auth/rembrandt

WEBMUSEUM: REMBRANDT

Rembrandt. Rembrandt HARMENSZOON VAN RIJN (b. July 15, 1606, Leiden
Neth. —d Oct 4 n1669 Amsterdam)
Short Bibliography of the greatest artist of the Dutch school

www.rembrandthuis.nl

MUSEUM HET REMBRANDTHUIS, AMSTERDAM

. . . for the Macromedia Flash Plugin. GO NON FLASH
Description: In the heart of old Amsterdam stands a small house with an oak
door and red shutters

www.mystudios.com/rembrandt/rembrandt-myself-opening

REMBRANDT – MYSELF

A look at Rembrandt's self portraits

Self Portrait Open Mouthed As If Shouting 1630

Self Portrait with Raised Sabre 1634

Self Portrait with a Velvet Cap with Plume 1638

Self Portrait as St Paul 1661

Would it help if I knew what Stanley looked like: would that help me build a picture of him? Of course not. So he's 6'3" and weighs 220 pounds. Does that make him a gentle giant or a big thug? Neither, it's what he does that counts.

What do I look like? I am Dogg and you'll never know. What do you look like? I don't know, but I also wonder whether you do. I mean, sure you recognize yourself in photographs, and in the mirror when you're brushing your teeth at night, but I bet you don't really believe either of these images is true. You can't get to the complete picture can you? The mirror image is reflected, the photo a memento mori. It all gets tricky for the I of the beholder. How can you ever know the truth about yourself, when your inner story is always shaping the facts the way it wants them?

You can't get rid of the credit card syndrome.

Take a self-portrait for instance. By Rembrandt. Is that the way he looked or is it the way he felt? Take the way he uses light, for instance. It's not uniform. Like he's shaping the facts, highlighting certain features, particulars of the personality. Is that more true than a photograph? Did old Harmenszoon van Rijn, with his squidgy nose, tell you more about himself than a photo would? He was letting the feeling come through the brushstrokes. Self-knowledge on canvas, letting you look in onto his soul.

Ah but was he telling the truth?

Finally, Rembrandt was Dutch, which reminds me of my last visit to the Netherlands. Memo to Dutch restaurateurs: figure out what 'well done' means. However, the Dogg must compliment the same on their excellent selection of various strains of marijuana. Nice hors d'oeuvres.

Digital Mind Modelling Project

The purpose of the Mindpixel project is to collect data to build a statistical model of an average human mind.

GAC [Generic Artificial Consciousness] is being created even as you read this. But 'he' needs you – or rather your mindpixels.

A mindpixel is a true/false statement that everyone [with half a brain] will answer the same way, such as 'deer have feathers'. By making a database of knowledge from squillions of facts, GAC will learn the basic questions necessary to human existence. You're teaching him what it is to be human.

<u>Stanley Rhodes File</u>

Stepney Housing Association

Tenant   Stanley Rhodes
Property   Flat C
                  14 Belfrew Road

Inventory

1 single bed, l mattress (stained), 2 pillows (foam)
1 bedside table (top chipped LHS)
1 table lamp, plug, cream shade (stained)
1 occasional wood table (surface scratched)
1 lightshade (cream)
1 wardrobe, mirror, misc hangers
1 chest of drawers (lower LH drawer handle missing)
2 framed prints (Monet, London)
1 wastebin, green metal
1 heater, night storage

Paintwork beige (patches under window)
Carpet cream (stains nr wardrobe, worn at doorway)

This Stanley guy is getting to me, messing with my mind. Take a look at the place he lives in. A skeleton of a room, beaten-up furniture, no TV. The guy's living in a cell still.

I'm going to have to draw the line. I mean a detective like me can't sit up all night listening to a mini-cab company controller calling out his troops.

However light the file, I decided I had to get it to the client straight away:

Subject: Stanley Rhodes

Dear Giselle

Your subject Stanley Rhodes is proving elusive. No – I'd go so far as to say he's a flatliner. Barely a data heartbeat. As you will probably know he's done time for drugs; now he's straight. No sign of a clientele show-ing up. In fact he's turned to religion as a better opiate. He works for a mini-cab company. Does nights. Never misses – although he did stop one last night after a fight with a punter who wouldn't pay the fare. No boozing. No spending other than essentials. No women. In fact noth-ing to get anyone excited about him. Like no-one would miss him if he wasn't there. Please let me know if you wish me to continue. Apologies for lack of detail. Dogg.

Subject: Stanley Rhodes

Dogg. You surpass yourself. But you're also holding out on me: give me the details on the fight Stanley got into. I know you can, you tease.

I will send you the basic information on the next subject I want you to tail soonest.

Giselle

OK, something untoward is going on here. There is a game being played around me. Why is this woman Giselle so thrilled when I give her nothing? I mean the report I filed on Stanley couldn't have been thinner. But she makes no comment. Gives me a slap on the back and then wants to know about Stanley's scuffle.

I can send her more details, but that doesn't get her or me off the hook. We're dealing in ex-cons here and either I find out what's going on or I give up the job. No-one's forcing me to take this stuff on. I can go back to the usual diet of missing persons and mating data – who's doing it to whom and how.

But hey, Dogg, why don't you admit it? You know you want to do it. You know that it's precisely because Giselle isn't being straight with you that you're putting far more effort into this little antic than the fee justifies. Come clean, Dogg. You want some adventure in your life. Data that takes you in dangerous territory. But you're not a complete fool, Dogg.

You take risks not chances.

So who is it you're working for?

01/02/02 10.41
Dr Giselle Jackson File

Bank Acct   Lloyds TSB
                      24 67 34 30304546

Lloyds MCard No. 4775 91802227 4176
Expires   08/02

last five CD purchases
HMV Oxford, 43/46 Cornmarket Street OX1 3HA
Lynne Shelby I Am   13.99
Gilberto Bebel Tanto T   13.99
Mariza Fado Em Mim   14.99
Cowboy Junkies Trin Sess   11.99
Mozart Violin Concerto   13.99

last 5 book purchases
Amazon.co.uk
No Logo: Naomi Klein   5.99
The Floating Brothel: Sian Rees   6.39
The Idea of Perfection: Kate Grenville   5.99
Sleeping Arrangements: Madeleine Wickham 5.99
Electric Light: Seamus Heaney   7.19

purchases over £1000 in last six months
Cassandra Goad: Designer and maker of fine jewellery
Garnet Apolloma Bracelet   £1740.00

www.softfactsdb.com

Little Known Facts Questionnaire:
LIVING ARRANGEMENT   House with thatched roof
WHAT BOOK ARE YOU READING   No Logo by ms klein
FAVOURITE BOARD GAME   Scrabble
FAVOURITE MAGAZINE   Hello (yes I admit it)
FAVOURITE SOUND   listening to the sea
WORST FEELING IN THE WORLD   Wishing you could speak to
                                      someone who's dead
WHAT IS MOST IMPORTANT   work (sad isn't it)
CHOCOLATE OR VANILLA   Chocolate
DO YOU LIKE DRIVING FAST   Yes
FAVOURITE ALCOHOLIC DRINK   Wine
IS THE GLASS HALF EMPTY/HALF FULL   Full
DO YOU SLEEP WITH A STUFFED ANIMAL I used to but now I'm single

Have done a quick and dirty check on the money files of my client Dr Giselle Jackson. She's comfortable. Taking in over £100,000 a year. From the odd spend profile I've done she seems a reasonably well-educated, well-formed thirty-something female.

Via a database mining company I picked up one of those chain-mail questionnaires she's filled in for a friend. Detect the odd sharp edge to her comments, like she's got a strong mind of her own. Not intimidated by men. Drives fast and close to the breaking point. She's obviously committed to her work, probably very driven. Would have to be earning the sort of money she is in her thirties.

Will have to wait for more data, before I make up my mind on this one, but the Dogg is intrigued.

www.bravissimo.com

This is a truly beautiful box set from the Queen's corsetieres, Rigby and Peller.
Go ahead and treat yourself to something really special.

Ref	RP 18	36D	Black	£50.00
	RP 20	L	Black	£29.00
	RP 19	L	Black	£29.00

This is one of the best fitting bras in the collection. Mocha is a great colour for
no show through, sheer or light clothes and Bordeaux is simply stunning.

Ref	FA 45	36D	Bordeaux	£30.00
	FA 46	L	Bordeaux	£15.00

Total   £153.00

Ms G Jackson
30/01/02 10 19.51   2472
Paid Lloyds Mcard   4775 91802227 4176 exp. 08/02

Back Size	Brief/Thong/Suspender/ Bikini Bottoms size	Dress Size
32	S	10
34	M	12
36	L	14
38	XL	16
40	2XL	18

Thought I'd share this little item from my trawl of the retail sites that Ms Giselle Jackson has been to in recent months. Buying underwear from bravissimo.com.

It always interests me when online searching throws up a different way of knowing someone. Shows how online identities are constructed, from the trivial as much as the significant fact. Indeed, often it's the trivial fact that gives insight on a person's inner story: who they believe themselves to be.

For instance, in this case almost the first thing I know about Ms Jackson is her taste in underwear. Secrets are revealed right from the first meeting, even before. You've seen the person half-naked and they don't even know it. You know intimate details about them while they are still on polite conversation. What's more, you get an idea about their sexuality and their attitude to sex, even before you shake hands. We know in this instance that Ms Jackson sees herself as desirable. Now that's inner story detail if ever I saw it.

File: Dr G. Jackson

Current employer:

Destiny Research Center
Thames Reach
Abingdon
Tel: 0118 4960000

Destiny Research: At the forefront of genetics research.

www.news.bbc.co.uk

The government wants to store the DNA of every person arrested in the UK.
Currently, police have 940,000 DNA samples in the national database. By
2004, the database should hold more than three million samples – equivalent
to 'almost the whole criminal class of the UK', Downing Street has claimed.

Giselle works for Destiny Research, a genetics outfit. We're talking succulent data now. The human juice. DNA.

DNA makes us both unique and the sum of our species. Each individual has different data, yet our file's a compilation of every generation stretching back to the ooze. Back to the beginning of cells. Isn't that amazing, I mean have you ever looked at your hand and thought this hand is mine, it's different to everybody else's, it's got a unique fingerprint and yet it's built from millions of hands across our whole descent. It is at once unique and species.

So DNA is the ultimate in dead men's data, alive on the files of the living. It's the past and the present. It's the whole stretch. And it's sure changing the face of detective work.

I mean this DNA fingerprinting, it provides the perfect fact in any investigation. No more 'maybe you were at the scene of the crime, maybe not'. This is incontrovertible evidence. That's new, boys! That's something we're going to have to come to terms with very fast. A certain fact. The Dogg loves it but also recognizes what it does for the human condition. It provides a fact that we can never explain away. No matter how much you plead your innocence, if the DNA matches, you're guilty. End of discussion. It's so absolute, it kind of takes away humanity's presumption of innocence.

Another thing DNA does for crime: it takes away motive. No need to establish motive any more. If the DNA matches, then you're IT.

Maybe Giselle has got some DNA from these subjects and is trying to match it to some long unsolved murder. And these days no-one's safe from conviction: you get copped and you're going to have to give in your little saliva sample. And they'll store that on a database – which the Dogg – like many another professional – will be happy to give his customers access to.

What's more, the police have got all this DNA on their database. Wonder what else they do with it?

DESTINY RESEARCH CENTER
THAMES REACH
ABINGDON
OXON

Directors: Dr J. Cowie, Dr G. Jackson, S. D. Franklin, Dr B. Abrahams
Senior Researchers: Dr S. Newman, J. Panton

Established 1998

www.destinyresearch.co.uk

The Center's stated aim is to become a centre of excellence in the field of applied genetics. Its expertise lies in genetic analysis and monitoring homogenous population groups. The Center is actively seeking new applications for its growing database.

For further information please e-mail us at info@destinyresearch.co.uk

From 1994 through 1999 the biotech industry raised a total of $30.9 billion in equity venture financing. In 2000 alone, the sector raised almost $13.4 billion on a global basis.

Leading Biotech Companies Ranked by 1999 Worldwide Sales:

1. Amgen $3,340m
2. Quest Diagnostics $2,205m
3. Quintiles $1,607m
4. Genentech $1,421m
5. Teva $1,282m

Over 4,000 diseases are known to involve some level of genetic cause.

Giselle's business goes way beyond DNA fingerprinting. Take a look at the website. It's got 'Do not disturb' written all over it. Very cool and carefully done, just lets you know their field of research, but not what they're actually doing to the mice in their cage.

But I know the mice. Personally. They're men on the run from something, running on the wheel of existence. And my role: I'm watching the experiment, timing them on the wheel, following them through the maze, tracking the decisions they make. Only I'm doing it for real. Under the ultimate lab conditions: everyday life. You have to hand it to Giselle, if you're going to run an experiment, what better way than to do it live; and with the Dogg watching on.

Can't help but salivate over what sort of genetic data Giselle holds on these guys. Guys like old Gerald and Stanley 'Flatliner'. If it's not simple DNA stuff – then it has to be more medical.

So far most of the stuff from the genome projects has been linking specific genes to certain illnesses – everything from acne to Huntington's Disease. There's the promise of massive advances in medical science. New cures for cancer and diabetes, just around the next genetic curve. And for the Dogg's money, he bets they're going to be right. Sure, the Dogg thinks genetics will change medicine entirely. Governments around the world are telling us they can't afford universal care: but that's because they're using industrial revolution (albeit very smart) technology to cure the human body. And that's very expensive. But what if genetics offers us the true, the genuine 'physician cure thyself' – that is, harnessing the natural technology of the body to heal itself? If this is so, we can grow cures. Medicine becomes cheap: 'Cure for cancer? Sure, just take two of these.' Yeah it's going to be so cheap that it's going to worry the hell out of governments and industry. They all say they want universal health care. But do they? Isn't cost a convenient excuse and reason: a reason for the medical industry and an excuse for mortality? Allowing people to die may be less expensive than allowing them to live.

The Dogg digresses. Can't see how any of these boffins would be interested in Stanley and Gerald. From the data I've gathered, their only common denominator is that they served time, but frustratingly not in the same prison. So where's the link?

DECODING THE HUMAN BODY

The secrets of life: It is the most expensive, most ambitious biology mission ever. The Human Genome Project at $250 million and counting is biology's moon shot. In the eyes of boosters, it promises to provide no less than the operating instructions for a human body, and will revolutionize the detection, prevention and treatment of conditions from cancer to depression to old age itself. In the eyes of critics, it threatens to undermine privacy and bring on 'genetic discrimination' in insurance and employment.

Sharon Begley Newsweek April 10 2000

www.sanger.ac.uk/info

To sequence the human genome (DNA)

Our DNA is made up of four base chemicals identified by the characters
A C G T

A typical DNA sequence may look similar to:

actgccagcagtctgttagcgccgaagcaggagattgctt
cagtactgtagcccgagaccagcctggcaacatagcgaa

Fascinating isn't it, that you and I are built from little bits of data. Six billion of them. All strung together by a code. The secret of life is a code. ACGT, combined in billions of ways. We're a sequence. We're blips, in little command chains that build proteins that build life.

But the big thing is — we're not a secret any more. The operating instructions are out. Yours and mine. And how are we going to cope with that? I mean someone like Giselle has the data on Stanley and Gerald. She's got the source code on these guys and she's watching them move around their cage. But what if right now, she and I were watching you? What if she had your genetic data, and you had no idea what use she was putting it to? Good or bad, commercial or altruistic.

Kind of worrying though.

Right now nobody's got the answers to these questions. That's why the establishment is moving in to try and control things. Like they did with the Internet and failed. But with this genetic stuff they're even more serious.

But again the Dogg says the secret is out. You can't control the genetic data. Information Wants to Be Free. And it will be free. There's no other way. The technology is there. Can't hold it back. You know, sometimes the Dogg thinks that the whole IT revolution happened just so that we'd have the technology in place to process the huge amounts of data being released by the genetics boffins. I mean these guys are peering into the innermost reaches of the human being, not with a microscope but a semiconductor. Harnessing massive data-processing power that was given its dry run helping poor little Industry improve on its stock control. If you think about it — all of this computing power is simply wasted on business and consumers and the education lobby. It's about synching up with bigger forces. 'The Truth is Out There' — yeah — but maybe more importantly 'It's Inside Here'. Inside You and Me. Sir Thomas Browne got it right, back in 1635: 'We carry with us the wonder we seeke without us.'

www.psychology.unn.ac.uk

HERITABILITY

The standard measure of the relative contribution of genes (as opposed to the environment) to a particular characteristic is called heritability.

Relationship	Genetic Similarity
Monozygotic (identical) twins	100%
Dizygotic (fraternal) twins	50%
Brother/sister	50%
Uncle/aunt/nephew/niece	25%
Half-brother/sister	25%
First cousin	12.5%
Second cousin	6.25%
Unrelated person	0%

We share data. Data is what makes us family. We're family software.

Funny how what's old becomes new. In the past family meant mutual responsibility. You looked after one another. Family gave protection.

In the genetics age, family means sharing very similar data. Similar data means your operating instructions are much the same, you share the same flaws. The natural consequence of this is that mutual responsibility comes back into fashion. Except that the protection you're now dealing with is not the threat from outside, but from within. The responsibility is about data. And whether you share knowledge about that data. If one of you tests positive for a particular disease, then there's going to be a whole big deal as to whether you tell the others in your family. Data sure is going to bring the family together again.

Maybe Gerald and Stanley share something more than a prison record.

Bioethics.net
The American Journal of Bioethics: where the world finds bioethics

Are you very worried about the possibility of discrimination or loss of privacy as a result of genetic research, somewhat worried, not too worried or not at all worried?

Very worried 19%
Somewhat worried 37%
Not too worried 23%
Not at all worried 20%
Don't know 1%

Do you think that the government should or should not regulate?

The uses of gene therapy that is altering genes to cure and prevent diseases
Yes should regulate 69%
No should not regulate 25%

The use of genetic therapy to pick traits in unborn children
Yes should regulate 50%
No should not regulate 44%

www.city-journal.org_html/10_1_dna_testing.html

Chris Hadkiss, the DNA manager for the Forensic Science Service in London, an independent lab that tests DNA for the police: 'It will not be long before police officers will be able to scan DNA evidence at a scene as easily as they check number plates.'

These days lots of people are wising up to the data industry, to the way in which their personal records are being bought and sold, analysed and mined for information. And that's worrying but most of us can probably live with it. You know, someone hacking into your credit card or bank account is going to get lots of valuable information on you, but hey, worse things happen at sea.

Well worse things are about to happen. The end of privacy has only just begun. The next stage isn't just about getting into your personal life, it's about getting into your life itself. Looking through your genetic data.

And please don't say that's not going to happen. Wise up.

Right now, the people most involved in genetic research are calling for laws to protect our genetic privacy. Come on, guys. Once the secrets have been discovered, nothing is going to stop them getting out. This is species information, you can't stop others in the species wanting access to it. Your data, the blood flowing round in your veins, will be mined and the patterns they discover are not necessarily going to be good news. The stuff that makes you and me, those 6 billion numbers. You think you own them? Dream on.

04/02/02   11.24

<u>Giselle Jackson File update</u>

<u>e-mail from giselle@destinyresearch.co.uk</u>

Dear Dogg

I now have the name of the third subject. Same profile same money.
Also could you let me know if our other two runners are up to anything new.

Best regards
Giselle

Well it didn't take Ms Giselle long to get back to me with another case. She's all fired up by what I'm giving her. Like I'm proving some theory.

That's fine. It's what the Dogg is paid to do. Provide facts, clear and clean, without the mess of emotions. I have to admit I admire her. Releasing the mice back into the wild and getting Dogg to track them. That's a stroke of genius. Most of these scientists want to hide behind the anonymity of their laboratory doors. 'Keep Out,' they say. 'You just won't understand what's going on.' And that way science gets itself into a lot of bother. Remember information wants to be free.

But Giselle's out there in the real world. And she's found the perfect combination, objective data from Dogg, like you'd get in a controlled experiment, matched by the truth of real life testing. No emotions, yet your theory is proved for real in the chaotic, random, emotional world, the only place anyone will ever genuinely prove their theory. One more set of data will really start to seal things for Giselle and she needs Dogg to gather it.

But I'm still puzzled by her method and why she's congratulating me on a good job on Stanley Flatliner, when all I've really uncovered is that he drives a mini-cab and had an argument with one of his customers?

I think you and I need to meet properly, Giselle.

Dr Giselle Jackson File

Giselle Francine Jackson
b. Bath 19/6/64

29 Houlton Close
Islip
Oxon OX7 3HA

Telephone	01632 960007
Nat. Ins. No.	TQ 7268422L
Nat. Health No.	296648251

Mobile	0777684329
e-mail	giselle@destinyresearch.co.uk
	giselle@riverso.co.uk

Parents:
Ronald David Jackson d. 12.4.97
Deirdre Alice Jackson b. 22.1.34 retired professor

Curriculum Vitae

1975–82	Royal High School, Bath
A Levels	Biology, chemistry, mathematics, general studies

1982–86   St Anne's College, Oxford
Biochemistry First Class Honours

1986–88 D Phil: 'Molecular characterisation of the orphan receptor pCHx1'

1988–90   St Hilda's College, Oxford
Junior Research Fellow, Dept of Biochemistry, Oxon

1991–4   University Lecturer, Dept of Biochemistry

1995–6   Médecins Sans Frontières

1997–98   Immu Biotech
Senior Researcher

1998–   Destiny Research

Current Salary

£120,000

Giselle is quite a package. A good example of the species. She's very intelligent. Straight 'A's all the way, took a first at Oxford and was the top science graduate of her year. She's sociable too: she was president of the JCR. She must have had presence and been liked well enough by her cynical siblings at St Anne's College.

Her undergraduate career was a great success and that achievement followed into postgraduate research. She did a D Phil in molecular biology and subsequently landed a good teaching job. In most people's opinions she would have had Oxford at her feet, the world at her feet.

She keeps this pace up for long enough to show that she's a serious contender in academia. Then, and here's the interesting part, she gives it all up. Takes a break not just from her work but from Britain too. She goes off to Africa of all places – doing a stint of voluntary work.

Now I guess we've seen this pattern before. Very bright young student is hot-housed into academia. Never has an adolescence. Never has a break, going from one challenge to the next. But sooner or later the gaskets blow. The career is based on intensity of focus; let that waver a little and the whole world falls apart. It was made of iron will, determination and ruthless ambition. What sets people like Giselle apart is will.

From the file so far, it seems that Giselle recharges her batteries in Africa doing good works and then comes back to the UK. This time she doesn't head for academia. She goes commercial. First a Biotech company and then starts up at Destiny Research.

So when she comes back, she goes for the money. Africa is where we all find a conscience, and where conscience finds food aid wagons looted and their grain sold on the black market.

Gerald John Keatring File

new data 04/02/02

Match <u>Gerald Keatring</u> to all databases

>>>>>>

Police National Crime Files
CAD (Computer Aided Dispatch) Report

RECORDED IN IR BY CC00875 AT 20:04 SERIAL 10187

REC BY: CCC:IR

PHONE

LOCATION: DE LA RUE CURRENCY, KINGSWAY, SOUTH WAY, TEAM VALLEY TRADING ESTATE, GATESHEAD, TYNE AND WEAR, NE11 0SQ

TYPE: 05\65

GRADE: I

CALLER

VRM

CLASS:

ASSIGN: W2, WY1, WY81, TJ421

TIME	USER ID	REMARKS
20.04.12	2298456	^ INFT STATES ARMED ROBBERY AT LOCN. REPORTS 4 SUSPECTS. BLVD GUNSHOT WOUND (LEG) TO 1 SUSPECT. <u>GERALD JOHN KEATRING</u> NFDS.
20.04.42	2298456	LOCAL UNIT TO ATTEND PLEASE

I was going to stick to Giselle's data plan, but something much more urgent has pressed for attention. Gerald's been arrested. You're with me in real time. Data hot off the screen.

He's been picked up in the process of doing a job on De La Rue. As they like to joke in the City of London, this is the company that 'has a licence to print money'. De La Rue produces Her Majesty's bank notes, and incidentally most people's cheque books. This is a major league robbery taking place.

It only had to be a matter of time before Gerald made his next job. In fact I'm pretty sure he's been knocking places over for a few months now, keeping his hand in, waiting for the big one. The spending profile I put together on him shows he's been getting in decent amounts in cash pretty regularly. Enough to splash out on presents and keep him in booze. But this one – well this job would have bought him more than just a few 36" screen colour TVs. This was a serious effort to get free of his past.

The only trouble with big time money is that it tends to be protected by big time security. By men with shooters and more importantly by other men behind the scenes who do the intelligence, gather the tip-offs, stop the crime before it ever takes place.

Sounds like it was that way at De La Rue. Gerald's taken a bullet in the leg. They were there waiting. The guys in black with bullet-proof vests. Night scopes, trained marksmen, there to take you out.

04/02/02

Queen Elizabeth Hospital
Gateshead
Tyne and Wear
NE10 9RW

Intensive Care Unit

Critical

Police Admittance
Gunshot wound.

Patient Profile: Gerald Keatring

Attending surgeon's notes.

Admitted at 23.47. Bullet wound in upper rt lung lobe 2.5–3 cm. Exit wound left of D5-6. Massive hemothorax. Patient resuscitated according to advanced trauma life support protocol. Full trauma activation called. Patient placed on life support machines. Two litres of haemorrhaged blood removed from chest cavity. Pulse very thready. Initially minimal blood pressure.

Immediate operative intervention. Rt lung removed. Further exploratory procedures.

Await further intervention.

Things are a lot worse for Gerald than I thought. The shot must have been bad. And he didn't take it in the leg either, as the initial police report suggested. It was a bullet to the chest. Exit wound just missed his vertebrae – which is maybe the only good news for Gerald so far. At least his spine is undamaged. Or that's how I'd guess.

First operation they took out his right lung. Massive bleeding. And that isn't the end of it. Obviously there's going to be a second operation.

The bullet entered his chest and went clean through. High velocity bullet. Official release weaponry. One shot too, so it was by marksmen; if it had been ordinary cops covering the De La Rue premises we'd have seen more peripheral damage, other wounds to the arm or leg. Splintered hands, bullets lodged in the abdomen. But this was a take-out.

Interesting to know if it was a set-up. Or just a blunder on someone's part. Anyone can do a break-in, but keeping your mouth shut about it before and after, well that's much more difficult. And of course once you've done one profile job, the boys in blue are going to be watching you ever afterwards: under surveillance.

http://spy.org.uk

CCTV operators are finally starting to register with the Data Protection Commissioner. However, to date fewer than 50 such CCTV operators have registered – all the other CCTV cameras in the UK are in breach of the Data Protection Act. Even if you think that you have a legitimate 'crime prevention' use for a CCTV system, you still need to register.

The only CCTV/Video Surveillance operators not breaking the law:

1. ARGYLL AND CLYDE HEALTH BOARD
2. BIRMINGHAM HEALTH AUTHORITY
3. BRIGHTON HEALTH CARE NHS TRUST

51. UNITED KINGDOM ATOMIC ENERGY AUTHORITY
52. UNIVERSITY OF PORTSMOUTH
53. VISA INTERNATIONAL SERVICES ASSOCIATION

http://www.kingshealth.com/services/security/menu

We monitor over 100 CCTV cameras.

We monitor Panic and Intruder alarms across the main hospital complex and satellites such as Dulwich Hospital, Mapother House and the clinic at 100 Denmark Hill.

http://cctvconsult.com

Free consulting page on Video Surveillance Cameras

This is the right place for you to get the answers you deserve.
This is where you can find your solution.

Hacking into CCTV systems has become a new pastime of mine. Simple enough – any camera connected to a computer is just waiting to be used. And the fun is that it gets you right in close. Right into the world – and you learn a whole new language. Like ARP: the Address Resolution Protocol which helps you match an IP (computer) address to a physical machine address. So you can select which camera you want to watch through. Then there's automatic iris – the diaphragm device in the lens that adjusts to light level changes, allowing you to get a clearer picture. And Field of View (FOV) gives you the width, height or diameter of the scene you're monitoring.

In my FOV right now is a bed. There's a guy on the bed with a load of tubes running into him. There's an oxygen mask over his face. Next to him no bedside light, but a stack of monitoring equipment.

Gerald is alone in the room with the equipment. The Dogg would guess there's a police guard on the door outside.

A light starts to flash on the stack beside Gerald.

Two people come into the room. Fast. Nurse and consultant. Then two more nurses. Their gestures rapid and intense. Close body language. The consultant with Gerald. Turns to the nurses. They're moving Gerald out. Fast. Out of my FOV.

QUEEN ELIZABETH HOSPITAL

Intensive Care Unit

Patient Profile: Gerald Keatring
Second Operative Intervention. Ligation of bleeding. Complications.

Pronounced dead. 4.03 p.m.

Strange feeling for the Dogg to be there at the moment of death. To witness that passing. The ultimate private moment.

The code is broken for Gerald. Or maybe it is that he slips back into his code. The source code of life. The data within you is dead and yet always alive. Buried alive.

The code which made Gerald, his genetic code, is not his. It is just a secret that he kept for a while. On loan from his parents and from their parents, stretching back into the ooze. If you've lived you've shared the secret. The touch of fire. The green fuse. That's all that can be said.

JOURNAL OF GENETIC THEORY VOL. 6 ISSUE 6

FROM WHAT WE ARE TO WHAT WE DO: SHIFTING THE FOCUS IN BEHAVIOURAL GENETICS

Dr G. Jackson, Dr S. Newman

Abstract:

This article reviews the rapidly developing and highly contentious field of research into how genetics affects behaviour [behavioural genomics]. There is an increasing emphasis on anti-social or dysfunctional behaviours, although in the majority of studies the methodological focus is on small but widely dispersed populations such as individual families from different countries. This bias owes much to the dominant biology based methodology that has characterized the research that led to the discovery of the genome and identification of individual genes. The authors argue that this methodology and its underlying assumptions are insufficiently oriented to the behaviours in question. It is time to shift the emphasis from gene based analyses to more behaviour and field based studies. The controversy surrounding the measuring and monitoring of behaviour should not deter scientists from further investigation.

www.journgentheory/abstracts.cc
Subscription rates individuals £30 per 6 issues, institutions £45.

PSYCHOLOGY BULLETIN 2000 NOV; 126[6]

Plomin R., Crabbe J.

Genetic and Developmental Psychiatry Research Centre, Kings College London, United Kingdom rplomin@iop.kcl.ac.uk

The authors predict that in a few years, many areas of psychology will be awash in specific genes responsible for the widespread influence of genetics on behaviour . . .

I haven't been in touch with Giselle yet. Can get mail to her soon. But in the meantime, the bots I have set working on her organization are turning up some news.

Giselle isn't just involved in genetics. We're talking work at the frontiers, and she's out riding fences. She's into behavioural genetics. The most controversial arena of them all. It's one thing to look into the operating instructions of the human body, quite another to get into the software that makes us do what we do.

Giselle's making the link between genes and behaviour. She's saying that we're all hardwired. Programmed to behave in certain ways. This is not information that sits comfortably with the human race. We like to think we're a tabula rasa, that we construct ourselves. Or that society constructs us. Such wonderful naiveté.

Then along come scientists like Giselle and say 'Hang on a minute. It's all in your genes.' The new geneticists and neuroscientists are telling us we don't have nearly as much choice as we thought we did. We are all pre-set.

And the Dogg, what does the Dogg think of this assumption? For it goes to the very heart of the Dogg's existence. Is the Dogg nothing more than a detective programme? Does the Dogg have 'investigator' written through him like a stick of rock? Does the Dogg have a source code?

It's enough to send you stir crazy, isn't it? But like I said we're going to have to come up with our own answers. There's no shying away from this. The secrets are being unravelled. Giselle is working away – not in the labs any more but out on the streets. We have to have an answer to the questions being raised. We have to have a reply. Forget privacy, forget protection. In the words of my good friend HAL: 'Daisy, Daisy, give me your answer do.'

I wonder if she knew more about Gerald than she was letting Dogg know. Maybe I should tell her about Gerald in every gory detail. See what comes back.

08/02/02   09.21

e-mail from giselle@destinyresearch.co.uk

Dear Dogg

Many thanks for your update on Gerald Keatring. Who fired first?

Giselle

The Dogg is not sure what Giselle is at. She doesn't seem surprised at Gerald's death. Like it was bound to happen. Can't make much sense of her comment 'Who fired first?' either. Except maybe she's saying that Gerald was some sort of psychopath – which I don't buy.

Of course if she had asked me to follow Gerald, to stick to the trail, rather than going off chasing info on Stanley, then I could give her more details. I could have been on Gerald's coat tails, I'd have stayed inside his mobile phone. But now all I have to go on are the official reports on the scene. Let that be a lesson to you, Dogg, to leave the files running.

I love that phrase by E. O. Wilson 'We're a negative waiting for a developing tray.' Is that it? Was Gerald always going to die like this, in a shoot-out with swag? Like we know how his story ends, we just don't know when. Is Giselle working at the when, predicting our fate?

Incidents where the police have felt it necessary to discharge weapons resulting in death or injuries to criminals.

19/07/2001	Metropolitan Police	Julian Hatter, aged 32, was fatally wounded by shots fired by a police officer on the balcony of flats at Marshall House, Brixton, shortly after 3 pm. click for more
16/07/2001	West Yorks Police	The incident began at 9.00 pm when a man threatened officers at Selby police station in North Yorkshire. The man left the scene and could not be found. He went to the psychiatric unit of Newton Lodge carrying what was reported as a large rifle. Armed police were called and he was shot in the hospital grounds. click for more
13/05/2001	Gwent Police	The shooting incident occurred just before 10.00 am in Newbridge, where an armed burglary had just taken place. The injured man was moved to Royal Gwent Hospital, with a suspected firearm wound to his shoulder. click for more
03/02/2002	Gateshead Police	Gerald Keatring, aged 35, was arrested along with two other suspects inside the premises of De La Rue and co, security printers. The three men were detained peaceably, but one, Keatring, suddenly reacted violently and was shot while reaching for his bag. Keatring was wounded and taken to hospital. click for more
12/02/2002	Metropolitan Police	At 7.55 pm tonight Metropolitan Police Service officers were called to J. Sainsbury, New Cross Road, London SE14 after reports that a man was armed with an axe or machete. The man was shot and taken to hospital. click for more

Call me old-fashioned, but there's something about a police report that always makes the Dogg's nerves tingle. My favourites are the US reports. In just a few lines, they get your pulse racing. Where else can you read such examples of poetic compression as this: 'An all points bulletin described the man as a white male, six feet three inches, 220 pounds, with silver gray hair, driving a 1971 light blue Cadillac . . .'

The reports in Britain are a little more prosaic, but nevertheless they too conjure the Dogg's imagination. Like the incident with the West Yorks Police in Selby. This disturbed young man walks into a police station, threatens a few officers, walks off – and what do the police do? They lose him. Outside their own station. I mean that's got to be a scene hasn't it? And it gets better. Later they find him wandering the grounds of a psychiatric unit and what do they do? They shoot him. Where's the logic? Why not just shoot him outside the police station and save everyone a load of time and angst? Of course the Dogg may be being entirely unfair to the officers concerned, for he has to admit on this occasion he does not have the data surrounding that sad incident in Selby. But in the case of Gerald's shooting, the Dogg knows rather more.

It seems like the police were tipped off. At least no-one inside the De La Rue building raised any alarms. The SWAT team just conveniently turned up. So who tipped them off? From reading the reports, it looks like the three suspects had given themselves up. They had realized they'd been nabbed and there was little point in a struggle. What happens next is unclear. It seems that as one of the officers was cuffing Gerald he went berserk, struggled free from the officer's grip and started to reach for a bag that lay on the ground. Another of the officers, seeing this happen, thought Gerald was going for a gun and shot him before he could reach it. Only problem was that there was no gun found in Gerald's holdall. The original report said that Gerald had been shot in the leg, when in fact he had been shot in the chest. What's more the medical file from the hospital suggests that the trajectory angle of the wound meant that the shot came from above. Not that consistent with the police report of a struggle on the ground is it? Of course the discrepancy with the original report might have been a typing error and angles of trajectory are notoriously difficult – but still makes you think doesn't it?

15/02/02   09.18

e-mail from giselle@destinyresearch.co.uk

Dogg

You've given me Gerald. For which many thanks. Got a new subject. Name is Shermyn Frazier. Same brief as before.

Giselle

'Same brief as before'. What Giselle really means is that the experiment continues. She's waiting for her revelation: that moment of scientific truth.

Truth. Is that truth? The truth of science that seems so complete, so integral, so there-to-be-found. Yet wait a few years, maybe a decade, and another discovery disproves your own.

Truth is trick. It's what you believe for a while.

Perhaps I will find my own revelation in the work Giselle is doing. The ultimate detective's tool, the human genome as the answer to all crime. Instead of making patterns from everyday data, I'll be reading them from the microscope.

The recently announced working draft of the human genome incorporates roughly 3 billion base pairs of DNA on 46 human chromosomes. Some 98 per cent of this DNA is of unknown function, so called junk DNA. But the remaining 2 per cent encodes our estimated 60,000 to 80,000 genes . . .

Further information from www.ncbi.nlm.nih.gov/disease

Junk DNA. Don't you just love that idea? Junk Code. I mean the absurdity of the situation. We make the biggest breakthrough in the history of science, we map the human genome, and what do we find? That 98 per cent of the data is junk, of no use or function.

Some clever white coats have seized upon this fact to show a) that there's nothing much to man after all and b) that God really is dead this time. ('I mean why would (an omniscient) God create DNA with junk in it?' If he's so almighty clever, why would he waste time like that?)

Well the Dogg would admit that right now the findings don't do much good for God's Total Quality Management record. But the Dogg is prepared to give the Big G some leeway on this. Show a little humility. Because it's the Dogg's bet that the 98 per cent isn't junk at all.

It's where the mystery lies. Or I suppose you could consider it another way: if 2 per cent seems to account for all our current functions, just imagine the potential locked up in the other 98 per cent. If we can invent microwave ovens, Polaroid cameras, Subbuteo football, plastic, hairdryers, non-stick frying pans, beverage holders, Candarel and decaffeinated coffee working on just 2 per cent – think what the future holds.

However you cut it, the Dogg is learning that when it comes to clues and data, it's all too easy to believe the answers lie in the obvious, the visible 2 per cent. You have to have the mental strength to go beyond the conventional data trail. There are patterns elsewhere. Subtler patterns that reveal the truth. So far in this investigation I have overlooked the Dogg's own rules: Treat all data equally. Everything is relevant.

I have assumed too much and too early. I have looked for the obvious. I have not opened my mind to the unimportant detail that reveals the deeper pattern.

15/02/02   11.34

<u>Shermyn Daniel Frazier File</u>

Shermyn Daniel Frazier
b. Maidstone, Kent 12/3/77

Nat. Ins. No.   FP 70224139T
Nat. Health No.   821349625

H.M. Prison Records

Prisoner No.   RT9316

Shermyn Daniel Frazier

Black: British

Released: 11/02/02 on probation

Conviction: Death by dangerous driving, motor theft,
                       criminal damage

Prisons   Pentonville (remand); Wandsworth (CAT B)

Prev. Convictions   None

Probation Officer   Mr J. Knight

Contact Address   164 Raeburn Court, Chargrove Estate,
                       Hackney, London

Education   Elm Park Grammar School, 1987–1995
                       3 A levels Mathematics, English, Geography

Last Employer   Inland Revenue
                       Administrative Assistant
                       Cheam Tax Office

Parents
Frances Jossiana Frazier (Harper) – caterer m. 24/5/1972
b.16/03/46 Kingston, Jamaica
Benjamin David Frazier – Senior Manager, Customs and Excise
b.12/09/43 Kingston, Jamaica
164 Raeburn Court, Chargrove Estate, Hackney, London
Brother Jason David Frazier b. 23/9/75 – engineer, current employer Wates
and Son

Giselle's new subject is a mixed-up kid. His basic data's all conflicting. Comes from a sensible home, starts work for the Inland Revenue, and then gets put in the slammer for three years for criminal damage. The pattern doesn't hold together.

The Dogg must question which one of these stories doesn't fit: the sensible young man or the criminal? Not the sort of thing even the Dogg is going to be able to answer until more data is uncovered. Need to build up a much more detailed picture to judge which parts of the pattern do and don't fit.

One thing the Dogg can't work out: what links all three subjects as far as my client Giselle is concerned. All three of them have been to jail. But not to the same jail. They've all served time in different joints, so it's hard for Dogg to see how they're connected to Giselle: other than that they all have a record.

So it has to be that Giselle is getting her original information from inside the prison system. Maybe some medical process that inmates have to go through.

Her newest recruit, Shermyn, has just been released from Wandsworth prison. Fresh out, which explains why Giselle said she had a third subject for me but has only just given me his name – she was waiting on his release. As I see it the process goes like this: the first lab work was done inside, where the subjects were easy to monitor. Now they're out in the open, she's got me tracking them digitally, getting the objective data. When she's got enough to prove her case, she'll go public.

Of course she could have used an ordinary private dick or some security firm. They could have tracked these characters in person and wouldn't have charged much more. But they wouldn't have given the same level of data that Dogg provides. They wouldn't have stuck to the facts; and they wouldn't have looked for the patterns.

WANDSWORTH PRISON RECORDS

Shermyn Frazier

Plea: innocent
Conviction: Death by dangerous driving, motor theft, criminal damage to property
Sentence: 4 years
Provisional release date 30/06/02

File notes
'Excellent disciplinary record, commenced law studies, early release recommended.'
Probation Officer: Joe Knight

A small break from the pattern. Whereas Gerald and Stanley were stone cold guilty and accepted it, Shermyn pleaded innocent. That's an interesting variation for Giselle.

Not sure how much genetic information Giselle has on these three – but let's assume that since they were in prison she's got anything she needs. So she has a constant: they were all convicted criminals. She has the genetic information, so she can search the genotypes for identical 'markers' and she's got this interesting variation: one of them 'thinks' he is innocent.

All sorts of fab possibilities start blowing out here. Does he think he's innocent because that is what he believes, or because he can't tell the difference between right and wrong? He thinks he's innocent because he doesn't know what guilty is. Or maybe he's lying to himself. Or maybe he really is innocent. Whatever variation, I can see the frisson it brings to Giselle's experiment. A most interesting variable. In fact, the other two are data for the experiment. Shermyn is the proof.

So how does his behaviour inside fit into the findings? Shermyn acts like a good citizen. Does all that's expected of him and for his pains gets out early. He even studies the law when he's inside. That's not that unusual: criminals become obsessed by the system which has entrapped them. Pity is, they don't prove their innocence before they're found guilty and then it's too late.

searching > > > > > > Shermyn Frazier

Press Cuttings

03/09/98

Hackney Gazette

'GIFTED' BLACK YOUTH JAILED. FAMILY CLAIM COVER UP.

Residents in the Chargrove Estate are planning a major demonstration this week to protest the innocence of Shermyn Frazier, 21, recently sentenced to four years imprisonment for death by dangerous driving, car theft and criminal damage. Jason Frazier, his brother, has led the campaign to clear Shermyn's name. 'We all know that if you're young and black and live on the Chargrove Estate, you're going to get a different kind of justice,' Jason said after Shermyn's conviction last Thursday. 'Shermyn is utterly innocent of the crimes he's been convicted of. In fact he's the victim. Like his family is the victim now. Shermyn was the one the police found unconscious and bleeding. Yet he's the one that's been put away. You must ask the police why, and why so many people know that this was another case of "police crime". They are the ones who should be in court right now.'

The Chargrove Estate has seen frequent racial disturbances in recent months with tempers boiling over at what residents see as heavy handed policing. The incident with Shermyn Frazier has incensed local residents who claim Shermyn was a 'hard working, clean living, gifted boy'. more

Headlines:

FOUND BLEEDING AND BEATEN. AND HE'S GUILTY!

POLICE 'MISLAY' WITNESS IN SHERMYN TRIAL

Decided to do a little searching around myself, check out the circumstances of Shermyn's crime. Start surfing in the 98 per cent territory and I come up with some basic search engine stuff that's attracting my interest more than a little.

There was a whole lot of noise around Shermyn's conviction. Get the feeling this case was probably mixed up with years of other resentment, going deep into the community. Never easy to know who's speaking sense on these occasions. It's what so often happens when the facts get mixed up with emotions. They've all been jumbled in a series of accusation and counter accusation. In the end, both sides don't know who to believe – and when that happens facts become useless. They're twisted to make a point, masked to prop up propaganda. Like you get those statistics: 'Black people are now 7.5 times more likely to be stopped and searched and 4 times more likely to be arrested than white people.' Yeah? Now that may sound deeply unjust – because that's how it's meant to sound. But who knows whether this fact is correct or not? Like all of these statements (usually made in TV and press interviews) it's unattributed. And even when attributed, there's always another contradictory fact that will be given to disprove it. Experts differ; the facts contradict because they are not true facts, simply statements of belief dressed up to sound like facts.

All this is a real dangerous activity. Because it undermines the sovereignty of facts, the power of facts to protect. If we cannot trust facts we cannot expect justice or order or community. Truth breaks down, becomes relative. Then all things will fall.

We have to stick to the facts. Do not become involved. Don't let emotions distort your judgement. Do you think that because Shermyn is black he is more likely to be innocent or guilty? You see how easy it is to take sides.

Police National Crime Files

No CAD ref. PC 4821GD LORING takes report at GD STN Office

This is a theft/TDA of a m/v from outside the victim's home address.

1) The victim reported to police that between 2030 hrs on 01JUN98 and 0750 hrs 02JUN98 he was inside his house in JAMESTON ROAD, W1 having left his car locked and secure directly outside his premises. The vehicle did not have an alarm fitted.

2) Upon going back to the vehicle this morning he found that it had gone. There was glass on the road.

3) The victim made enqs with local residents but no witnesses traced. No CCTV at location.

4) Vehicle circulated as LOS on PNC, not known to London Trace folio 748224/02JAN02. No further enquiries until this vehicle is found. <u>Entered by 4821GD LORING at 1032 02JUN98.</u>

CAD 58394 refers, PC 6742GD GRAVENEY & PC 6821GD ROGERS attend

This vehicle has now been involved in a serious RTA on GD section. Police were called on the above CAD at 0201 hrs to a PI accident at the JB HABIB off licence, BOWLING RD, N2. Upon arrival of police a red Peugeot 205, index AB51DVL was found to have been crashed into the premises causing serious damage to the premises. A female pedestrian was apparently caught between the vehicle and the premises when the impact occurred resulting in serious injuries. LAS called (B401, B302 in attendance) but this victim was pronounced dead at the scene. She has been taken to Royal London Hospital. This victim has now been identified as ROSEMARY WALLACE of no fixed abode (HOSP report 06/98 refers).

cont . . .

Downloading the police files on Shermyn's incident. So far, we've got nothing to link Shermyn with the original theft of the vehicle.

More details are coming in.

cont . . . SUSP1, a male IC3, 20 yrs, was found seated behind the wheel by 6742GD and 6821GD, apparently unconscious. He was found to have minor lacerations to his face and what appeared to be a broken nose. He smelt of intoxicating liquor. He was conveyed to Royal London Hospital accompanied by 6742GD. A half-finished bottle of whisky was found by 6821GD on the back seat of the vehicle and has been seized as evidence (66/104/GD/98 refers). There is no evidence to suggest that any other vehicle was involved in this accident. This suspect will be required to give blood at the hospital and will be arrested as soon as he regains consciousness for the TDA, death by dangerous driving and criminal damage.

VIW1, Mrs ESTHER RAYE, was spoken to by 6821GD at the scene. She has given her address as 32 Falsham Avenue. She stated that she had seen the same vehicle shortly before the accident containing four young males. She stated 'They turned the corner going bloody fast, then I hear this crash and they were gone when I next looked. They must have crashed into poor Rosy whilst she was sitting in the shop entrance.' The descriptions of the occupants of the vehicle seen by VIW1 are poor and she was not sure of even an IC code when asked. Also asked if the vehicle seen by her to turn the corner was the same that had since crashed she stated 'Yeah well might have been'. Further to this, witness had clearly been drinking. The witness will attend GD Stn Office tomorrow to make a statement.

The vehicle has been removed for forensic examination, SOCO to pay attention to blood stains on the dashboard please. <u>Entered by 6821GD Rogers at 0455 03JUN98</u>

VIW1, Mrs RAYE, failed to turn up today to make her statement. I have visited her home address and spoke to the occupier Mr ANDREWS who told me that he has lived there for 4 years and has never heard of Mrs RAYE. Unfortunately we have no further means of contacting the witness.

The suspect was arrested this morning for the offences noted above by 6742GD (custody 58/GD/98 refers). He was required to give a sample of blood for analysis and this has been sent to the lab. He was bailed to GD on 07JUN98 at 0930 pending the results of the analysis. Entered by 6821GD ROGERS at 2125 03JUN98. The suspect returned on bail today and was interviewed regarding the offences. Lab results show 79 mgms alcohol from his sample and also traces of ecstasy. The suspect's blood has also been matched to that of the blood on the dashboard of the vehicle. There is no CCTV at the scene as the camera has been vandalized.

SUSP1 was charged by 6821GD at 1057 hrs for death by dangerous driving, criminal damage and TDA to which he made no reply. Bailed to appear before Bow Street Magistrates on 15JUN98 at 0930 (URN 01GD/72463/032 refers). <u>Entered by 6821GD ROGERS at 1142 07JUN98</u>

From the detail of the reports the facts only point one way, and that's straight at Shermyn. The Dogg can quite understand why the conviction went against him. Advice to drivers involved in car crashes: don't get caught with traces of banned substances in your bloodstream. For most judges, alcohol is one thing, but E is entirely another.

And then there's the little matter of a half-finished bottle of whisky in the back seat. Not a helpful detail.

Furthermore, the DNA tests confirm that it was Shermyn's blood on the dashboard of the car.

But of course there's the coup de grace, a woman was killed in the accident. Rosemary Wallace, 'of no fixed abode' as the police report puts it, was a female tramp who worked the area and had the misfortune to pick the wrong place to sleep that night. Fortunately she died instantly.

The only confusion is the witness statement. Why does she remember four people driving in the car when Shermyn was found alone at the wheel? Did his mates scarper after the accident and leave Shermyn to take the rap? If so, doesn't make Shermyn any less guilty does it? Not that the police appear to have tried to take the witness statement all that seriously – that comment in the report 'witness had clearly been drinking' seems a little heavy handed, like they didn't want anyone muddying the waters. Anyway the fact is that witness gave a false address and so presumably disappeared. Couldn't give her testimony to the judge hearing Shermyn's case. So her words, her version of the events simply don't matter. And if we are to take account of them now, we'd have to know what she really meant by that phrase 'Yeah well might have been.' I mean give that phrase to any half-decent TV actress and she'll give you eight or nine different interpretations. The woman could have had poor recall or been bullied into changing her mind by impatient police officers. But that's conjecture. Stick to the facts.

Officers present PC David Rogers and PC Amanda Whiteley

PC Rogers: In your own time, Shermyn, describe what happened to you the night of 3RD JUNE.

Shermyn Frazier: I had been out that night at a club – the Cube – and had a few beers. My girlfriend had ditched me the week before and I was feeling pretty sore about it. So I was in this club with a couple of mates and we started to chat to this girl. She seemed pretty friendly and when my mates went off to talk to someone else I stuck around with her. Shit I didn't realize that she was already with someone else in the club. Then this white bloke and his mates came up to us and start saying things like why am I messing around with white girls. And then his mates arrive and they start coming on strong, right, and doing some pushing and stuff so I reckon it's time to leave. Can't see my mates anywhere now so I decide to walk home on my own.

I get out of the club and I've been walking for a few minutes when I hear this car behind me. It starts blowing its horn and I think it's maybe my mates come to find me – I look round and I see this car coming straight at me and at first I think they're just larking around and then I realize it's the guys I had a bust-up with in the club and they're not going to stop and I panic and try to run and slip on the kerb. I'm getting up but the car's right on top of me, it swerves and the wing of the car catches me on the side of the head as I'm trying to get to my feet and then I don't know what happened. Next thing I know I'm in some hospital bed with a sore head, broken nose and a hangover. That's the honest truth. I don't know anything about the car or how I got there. The guys from inside the club must have put me there.

PC Rogers: Can you describe any of the people from the club who you say were in the car?

Shermyn Frazier: I can't remember too much about anything to be honest. One of the white blokes, the guy I thought must have been the boyfriend, was wearing a white T shirt, jeans and some kind of bomber jacket. The other guys were in just like shirts and jeans too. It was all pretty dark inside the club and I didn't want to hang around if you know what I mean.

PC Rogers: And can you explain how you came to be inside the vehicle and how your fingerprints were found on the steering wheel and dashboard?

Shermyn Frazier: All I can say is that somebody must've picked me up and put me inside. I wasn't driving the car. They must have put my hands on the wheel . . .

Shermyn is claiming it was a set-up. The jealous guys from the club try to run him down, but end up hitting someone else. When they realize what they've done, they shove Shermyn in the car and let him take the rap.

All very neat.

In fact quite persuasive. Shermyn has no previous record; he's got a good job. Why would he go out stealing cars and running them into late night shops? For fun, a boys' night out? If that's the case you'd expect there would have been someone else in the car with him when it crashed.

The key then to all of this is the witness. Unfortunately she disappears. If we believe Shermyn then she was frightened off either by the police or more likely by the gang from the club who were driving the car. But that's a real big if. There's no evidence to support Shermyn's story. It was his blood that was found on the dashboard. It was Shermyn that the police found slumped at the wheel of the car.

VOICES FROM FORGOTTEN VICTIMS – DEDICATED TO INNOCENT FAMILY MEMBERS OF PRISON INMATES

The purpose of this page is to provide a gathering place for all the forgotten victims to share their experiences, fears, hopes and dreams with others in the same situation. It is also my hope that those visitors who have never had a loved one in prison will leave with a new perspective of what it really feels like to 'Do Time With a Loved One'. You may even leave with a new friend.

You are listening to 'It Matters to Me' by Faith Hill – BECAUSE MY BROTHER SHERMYN MATTERS A GREAT DEAL TO ME and YOU MATTER TO ME.

Please take a moment to visit some of the websites in the 'Families Doing Time Together' webring. If you are a family member of a prisoner, and you have a website, please consider joining today.

WE ARE FAMILY. WHEN ONE SUFFERS WE ALL SUFFER.

Shermyn is innocent

click here if you want to help Shermyn Frazier – with information, support or just your love.

Update . . .

In the Words of Martin Luther King – Free At Last. Free At Last. Thank God Almighty Free At Last

The search engine bots are still bringing some tasty scraps on Shermyn – and I particularly like this one. A website started by Shermyn's brother Jason. Love the way that Jason posts a song for you to listen to while you're reading through the list of innocent victims. Real sticky.

Sites like this just go to show that if you share data you feel better. Information wants to be shared. The Web can heal. It's a transmission system that brings people together. In this fragmented world, it's also a support system. For Jason, the site was a way of dealing with his brother's sentence – and looks like he's going to keep it running now that Shermyn's been released. Still he probably means well.

Valete

After 23 years with the Force, PC David Rogers is taking early retirement. All those who want to wish him and his wife Pam well for the future are invited to the Barker Rooms, Mere Park Hotel, at 7.30 on Thursday 18th November.

www.metpol/intern/confident/rogers

Officer 6821GD
Rogers David

Confidential: recommended early retirement. Ongoing internal investigation into allegations of racial discrimination closed. No formal charges. Not proceed.

Took a look inside some Met police databases. Some interesting items that turn the facts a little Shermyn's way. Like I always say: 'It's what information, when'. The 'when' matters – if you and I had known from the outset that the investigating officer in Shermyn's case had been accused of racial discrimination, we'd probably have listened a little more attentively to his protestations of innocence.

Of course PC Rogers hasn't been convicted of racial discrimination. It's just that his early retirement makes him look more guilty than innocent. But that's making a lot of presumptions: he may have become ill, his wife may be ill, or he may simply want to play eighteen holes of golf three times a week while he still can.

And even if we knew that PC Rogers was guilty of discrimination that wouldn't prove he set Shermyn up on this occasion. Without a witness we've got nothing. Makes you think that CCTV might not be such an invasion of privacy after all, doesn't it? If the camera had been work-ing, in this instance, we would have known one way or the other. Absent such facts, the boy's still guilty as charged. But the Dogg will keep looking for other clues.

25/02/02 17.22

Online Application
Accountancy/Bookkeeping

Name	Shermyn Daniel Frazier
D O B	12 3 1977
Address	164 Raeburn Court, Chargrove Estate, Hackney London N19
e-mail address	shermynf@innocenti.co.uk
NI number	FP 70224139T
Education:	Elm Park Grammar School 1987–1995 9 O levels, 3 A levels
Snapshot CV	1996 Admin. Asst Inland Revenue 1997 Admin. Officer Inland Revenue 1999 Travelling
Current Status	Unemployed

15 second summary:

Have greatly enjoyed the last 2 years travelling the world, learning about other cultures and people. Now ready to put my accountancy/Inland Revenue skills to work in a commercial environment.

Back to the now. This job application turned up on a routine trawl through the Net, just a simple match for 'Shermyn Frazier'. But the implications are far from simple. First Shermyn is going straight. Looking for a decent job. Trying to forget his recent past. Second he's prepared to lie about it – well I guess he'd say that the best way to treat his stretch in jail is to say that it didn't happen. So if he fails to mention it on the CV now – it's simply because for Shermyn it didn't happen. Like he said, he was just 'travelling' for a couple of years. Loads of middle-class young kids go travelling for a while; see the world, travel broadens the mind etc. etc. Perfectly credible that Shermyn was just another of these travellers. And you know, maybe Shermyn will get away with it – and win the job.

Wouldn't anyone lie in such circumstances? In fact is it lying at all? We are all constantly shaping other people's perceptions of our identities through what we decide to tell them. Nothing wrong in that.

Shermyn is simply constructing his own data, taking charge of his own narrative, shaping his personal file with his inner story version of the facts.

Then something catches the Dogg's attention. The advertising banner above Shermyn's application, at the top of the jobs page.

It was to me an epiphany.

ARE YOU YOUR CAREER'S OWN WORST ENEMY?

Are you blocking your own chances of realizing your true potential? Psychologists have a word for it: they call it self-sabotage, the urge to wreck your own chances. Take the Top Jobs test and find out if you're a secret self-saboteur.

Self-sabotage. The phrase slices open an insight into this generation. This is the generation of those who have online identities. The first generation who are having to live with the consequences of database access speeds measured in nano-seconds. Allow one false fact to get recorded on the wrong database and hey, it's self-sabotage. SELF-sabotage. Warning: you have to take responsibility for the data on your file.

The implications of this go even deeper. Because so much information 'exists' on your file, and because this information is available instantaneously, it can take on a life of its own. It becomes a person, created from your personal data. Pretty soon it's competing for your personal space, competing for your narrative. After all, it knows everything about you, from your date of birth to where you live to who you phoned last night.

Of course this other you, this other narrative, will sound like you, look like you, talk like you. It's a double agent. And the more source code that exists on your file, the more perfect the match will be. But this data double is not a clone. There are tiny differences between the two of you, which would not be apparent to most people. Trouble is you know they are there, you know that the data double is an impostor. A doppelgänger with almost perfect recall, taking over your narrative. And what's more the impostor has all the weight of credibility on its side. The government, police, big business, credit card companies, life assurance firms – they all maintain that the real you is the one that exists on files, because that's the only one that they have ever met or indeed need to meet. (Furthermore, they need this data double to be the true you, otherwise their whole system falls apart.) In contrast, the only person who has met the internal you is – you! So who's going to believe little you? Case closed, your honour. The data double wins every time.

Believe me, there's a battle for identity going on. Your identity.

Our Genome Unveiled

Where do our genes come from? Mostly from the distant evolutionary past.

In a world where everyone can be known, accessed on global directory enquiries, we are becoming the facts others print out about us. Consequence: you may become trapped in the wrong data. An error gets on your file and comes to define you. Like Shermyn you claim you are innocent, even though the file may say you're guilty. And we know who will be believed.

Now perhaps that doesn't scare you. You think you're above it all: 'This guy Dogg is getting all worked up about . . . facts on a file! Yeah, right!' You don't care what others say about you. You're confident your internal story will prevail. Of course you could just be suffering from credit card syndrome. Even so the Dogg can understand your stance, and the Dogg might even admire your obduracy. Until that is, he starts to think about the new dimension the genetic data that Giselle is working on brings.

Add that to your file and see what happens, guys. The genetic stuff will truly blow your internal story away. There will be no more internal story. For we will know, as the advertising banner has it, our true potential. We'll be able to carry it around with us on a CD. Our genetic information burned into a disc others can play.

'True potential' – realize your true potential. That's the great hope which keeps mankind alive. That we have the divine within us, a secret spring which only the individual knows. And with this secret spring comes the belief that we can exceed the shackles of our environment, our education, our status. Man and Superman. All things are possible. We have the need to dream.

But what if, some time, man could unravel his and her evolution, interpret the genetic data and discover that there is no true potential? Or rather that the truth about your potential is that you've reached it: 'This is as good as it gets. You may say you're generous but the data says you've got mean genes.' What would this do to our dream dimension? What would this do to our sanity, when we hear the inner story no more? Will we go mad at the entrapment? We may have no choice.

LIBRARY OF POSTHUMANITY

We are no longer human – are you ready?

Bioinformatics may be defined as the use of computational and mathematical methods for the acquisition, archiving, and analysis of biological information to determine biological functions and mechanisms, as well as their applications. In practice it is concerned with such problems as
   – storing and annotating DNA and protein sequences
   – analysing sequence data to look for homologies between distinct sequences, or for gene regulatory or coding subsequences . . .

Bioinformatics and Biometry: David Balding

The bioinformatics market will soon exceed $1 billion per year.

Nature 15 February 2001

www.roche.com

SOON IT WILL BE POSSIBLE TO ANALYSE THE ENTIRE GENOME ON A SINGLE MICROCHIP

DNA (gene) microchips not only allow miniaturized automated test series to be set up, but can also analyse thousands of genes simultaneously. read the entire facet

What if the genetic data were to take a step further and disprove your internal narrative completely? Render it impossible. Who would you be then, my love, my sweet? We have all heard the words, 'You're not the person I thought you were', or 'I never knew you at all', but they take on a kind of spooky new meaning in this emerging arena of genetic data, don't they?

The Dogg is beginning to think that internal narrative will be squeezed out by two forces coming together: external facts and genetic data. And the effect of these two forces closing in from opposing directions is that there will be no room for argument. There will be proof. You'll have to accept the data. In future, there will be no strangers. Everything will be known about you. You can't just move to the next town and start again. The facts follow you everywhere. On your own CD which you'll carry with you, plug in, play and get 'treated'.

The myth of the inner story will be just a myth and you will know at last what frightens you. That you will know yourself and not like what you find. Worse, you will feel there is no man behind the iron mask. Simply the iron mask.

You are nothing but a set of instructions. Is that right, Dogg? Is your inner story just a code? The link between you and the music of the spheres is simply the incidence of intervals. Pure maths. Are you just a soft machine, Dogg? Or perhaps a machine that's gone soft.

28/02/02

<u>Shermyn Frazier File</u>

<u>www.fish4jobs.com</u>

Online Confirmation

Interview acceptance

Candidate   Shermyn Frazier

Placement   London Acoustic Centre

Position   Accounting Assistant

Date   27.02.02

Interview Notes
Interviewee was smartly dressed, alert and enthusiastic. Showed interest in business and is clearly capable with regard to accounting practices. Recommended.
J. Algar

Well someone believes in Shermyn. He's got that job he was applying for. So either they didn't check too much or he did a good job in the interview. Incidentally the notes on his interview file suggest he's an intelligent, upstanding young man. Comments about him were pretty favourable and they must have realized that if he'd worked for a couple of years with the Inland Revenue he could be a big help to them with their returns. Might even save them some money.

It was time to make my first report back to Giselle.

I gave her the gen on Shermyn: how he's just out of the slammer. How he pleaded innocent to the charges and how his family have supported him throughout the whole nasty business.

I also told her about the job and that Shermyn was rather economical with the truth in his application form.

In fact I said to Giselle: '*In Shermyn's case it looks as if he has decided to begin again, to start his life over. Well everyone has the right to expect to be given a second chance.*'

28/02/02   12.31

e-mail from giselle@destinyresearch.co.uk

Dear Dogg

So you think we all have a right to a second chance do you? Now if you'd said 'we all get what's coming to us' I'd agree. But Dogg, don't go soft on me and talk about fairness. You of all people should know that the world is not fair.

Anyway, Dogg, thank you for the update. Please continue surveillance on Mr Frazier.

G

I thought my comments were fairly innocuous. Didn't expect Giselle to get all fired up about them. I had touched a nerve all right. Giselle's reaction to my note was short and elliptic, but there was more edge than usual. I'd expected her to react more to the stuff I had found out about Shermyn's job application and the fact that he'd lied about his past. But that hadn't apparently interested her. What had caught her attention was a simple phrase like 'second chance'. Her reaction was out of line. Disturbed even, as though there was some wound I'd touched and it was bare and open and would not heal. That was one thing. The other element that surprised me was her goading. She wanted to draw me on, wanted me to get involved. She was asking me to cross the line.

When I started out in this business I wrote down a few simple rules for myself: Bye Laws for the Dogg Agency. These were adapted from the Good Girls' Guide to Survival on the Street:

1. Never return a kiss (don't get involved with clients)
2. Payment before pleasure (always get your money upfront)
3. Good girls like precautions (put a thin layer of anonymity between yourself and the client; never let them breach your first line of identity)
4. They know what they want, you know what they need (always stay one step ahead of the client; you always know more than they do)
5. All fantasy is private (don't confuse their world for yours; don't step over the line)

Tacky, but these rules had served me well. Kept me in business in the online world. Now I was in danger. A 'Miss Whiplash' kind of danger. 'Miss Whiplash' is saying, 'Come in here – if you dare, Mr Dogg.' She's tempting me to cross the line, become involved in other people's fantasies. And like all fantasies the lure is the promise of self-knowledge. 'Do you like it like this, Dogg? Oh you didn't know you did? Oh I see – and you've been alive for how long? What a sheltered life . . .'

CONFERENCE EXPLORES WHAT IT MEANS TO BE HUMAN

Perhaps one of the defining features of human beings is to ask the questions 'Who am I? Where did I come from? Why am I here? Where am I going?' Virtually all the peoples of the Earth have ancient stories that offer answers to these questions. These stories are embodied not only in narratives but also in dance and song and in forms of visual art and have often been a central element of religious lore and ritual practice. These stories both reflect and help to propagate broader understandings of what the world in which humans live is like.

Today advances in scientific understanding in many fields are providing new understandings of the world and new answers to these primordial questions . . . The mapping of the human genome is providing insight into both the contemporary biological constitution of human beings and also their evolutionary heritage. The dynamic relationship between human genes and human behaviour is becoming clearer. While genes may not directly determine complex personal and social behaviour, they do appear to establish behavioural propensities . . . Current developments in robotics and artificial intelligence represent an effort to constitute a human-like form of cognitive being in a non-biological form. Such intelligent robots have been called 'humanity's mind children'.

I have found myself asking these questions many times. Who am I? Where did I come from? I suspect we all indulge in them on occasion; poets more often. But like the guy says, it's only human; written into our species narrative.

Two things strike the Dogg about this assertion.

First, the Dogg suspects we are prepared to ask these questions because we know we'll never actually get the answer. We cannot know for sure, but we love to indulge in speculation. It's part of our need to dream.

But things are changing. The evidence is mounting. Detectives in white coats are out there tracking down the clues, following the leads, settling on a suspect. Soon they may know the answer, and what will we do then? For if one, only one, of us knows the answer, then we shall all know. We are in this together, though we have not given our consent to be so. We have not signed up to know, yet if one member of the team knows we will too. We are connected. Don't think you're not involved.

And my second observation: is this the ultimate test for human versus AI? Both human and computer can cope with the question, Who am I? But only one can cope with the answer. The computer.

Get back to work, Dogg. Remember, 'Arbeit Macht Frei'.

01/03/02   01.59

Giselle Jackson File

Dr Giselle Jackson
St Hilda's College Oxford

12/12/94   Resignation accepted from Dr Giselle Jackson. Immediate
              departure agreed.

MÉDECINS SANS FRONTIÈRES

14/01/95

Dr Giselle Jackson: Aid Worker
Project: Angola, general assistance, administration, medical
                      back-up

It was a group of exasperated French doctors who lit the spark which became
Médecins Sans Frontières. Frustrated and angered by the inadequacies they
saw in the global response to the Biafran Crisis in the 70s, they were
determined to create a unity of people – medical professionals, and logistics
experts – who, together, could bring humanitarian aid to whoever needed it,
anywhere in the world.

'Having been with MSF in some of the most extreme situations on earth, I
can't imagine working for anyone else. Their professionalism and humane
spirit inspire me. I don't know of any other medical organization that's
prepared to speak out for people in the way MSF does.' Thérèse Martin,
Paediatrician.

MEDICAL RECORDS

Dr S. Houtt. Plane Street, Oxford
Giselle Jackson file 15/01/95

Patient departing Angola imminent
Vaccinations: yellow fever (cert. issued), diphtheria, BCG, Hep A
Anti-malaria: Mefloquine; prevention methods discussed.

That gap in Shermyn's CV. It reminded me of another gap – in Giselle's career. There was something that didn't fit about it. She's working as an academic. Focused, successful, hell bent on reaching the top. Then just when she should be taking the step up to the big league, doesn't just quit her post, but the whole profession. Walks out and takes a year off to go to Africa.

www.msf.org

AGENCY CONDEMNS 'NEAR TOTAL NEGLECT' OF ANGOLANS

On November 2, the international medical relief agency, Médecins Sans Frontières, issued a scathing condemnation of the neglect of basic health-care needs of the population of Angola. The plainly worded document, prepared by aid worker Giselle Jackson, accuses both warring parties in the country's long running civil dispute of 'turning a blind eye to the obvious serious and often acute humanitarian needs of the Angolan people'.

For the past 26 years, the country has been devastated by a bitter civil war between the government and the rebel forces of the National Union for Total Independence of Angola.

Giselle disappeared into Africa for a year. Not a comfortable part of Africa either, she went to Angola. Home of the world's longest running, most savage war. Where they plant fields with landmines rather than crops. Angola – officially described by UNICEF as 'the worst place in the world to be a child'.

Giselle went there with Médecins Sans Frontières, so she was going to be right up there with the front line. She was going to see action all right, because those guys at MSF are usually the first in and the last out of any conflict. Where others fear to tread, MSF carry stretchers.

All of this sounds way out of character for our high-flying Oxford academic; the Dogg is sure that the Senior Common Room would not approve. But one thing does ring true: Giselle didn't pull any punches while she's out there. She wrote a report which cut a swathe through the hypocrisy of the conflict. She tried to bring those responsible to task. Dogg can imagine how it went: fresh, young, principled European woman comes face to face with the dark heart of Africa; the purposelessness of suffering. She feels impelled to do something about suffering that speaks in such words: 'In Mussende lots of people are dying of sickness, vomiting and diarrhoea, and swelling . . . I was sick and had no family. I could not go to the lavras (fields) because UNITA had laid new mines to stop people from returning to the fields to collect food. My niece had her leg blown off from a mine . . . while trying to collect food.'

This was the mad, violent world that Giselle inhabited for a year. As far from the cloisters of Oxford as she could go. With her knowledge of genetics, and the patterns of our DNA, Giselle must have asked herself – how did it all come to this?

OXFORD UNIVERSITY
DOMINUS ILLUMINATIO MEA

GENETICS DEPARTMENT

Michaelmas Term 1994

Department Submission to Research Assessment Exercise
Author: Professor Douglas Wright – Head of Department
Dr Giselle Jackson: Not selected. Teaching member of staff.

The Dogg must declare at this point he is interested in Giselle. Intrigued by her.

He likes the way she teases the Dogg. Tempting him to come on to the case, beckoning him over the line. The Dogg is perhaps even a little flattered that someone as obviously capable as Giselle should seek the Dogg's help.

It comes therefore as something of a surprise that Giselle was sacked from her post at Oxford. They didn't push her out of the door, but as good as. Her departmental head gave her the biggest possible academic thumbs down going: 'Not Selected' in her Research Assessment Exercise. On checking this out I have discovered that the Research Assessment Exercise is the way that academic departments announce their activities to the world – and is thus the primary means of establishing credibility and attracting funding. If you're not part of this showcase, then you've simply no worth to the department. In effect they're saying you're useless to them.

But it gets worse.

This sort of rating is rare. For those who work in the cloistered environment of Oxbridge colleges it's the kiss of death. Because it stays on your record, for ever. Try getting a job with this on your CV and you can forget it. A bit like having a criminal record you could say.

Oh and the final insult. Giselle worked in research. The head of department puts her down for a teaching post. I think we can safely assume he never wanted her to work in research again.

the ultimate press cuttings database

>>>search all references to <u>Giselle Jackson</u>

>>>dates   01/01/94 to 01/12/94

>>>national press

>>>local press

searching

GISELLE JACKSON

Bank Acct   Midland Current Account
                             30-16-90   79244186

01/01/94 Start Balance   £3,412.61

Payments in over £1,000 excluding salary [2]

£1,600 – 01/03/94
18/12/94 End Balance   £5,267.25

Midland Savings Acct
30-16-90   79244186
01/01/94   £9,807.50
18/12/94   £13,410.67

withdrawals   0
payments in   4   high £1,600; low £500

Philip Marlowe, private investigator, would have had a contact, a known face at the local newspaper who would have given him the inside story on this 'dame'. Me, I have a bot which scans all the pages of all the newspapers printed, in less than a second. Do I do a better job than Marlowe? Not for me to say. The difference is that I have to synthesize thousands of pieces of information into a single track; Marlowe had just one lead to go on from the start.

Trouble is we can both come up against dead ends. There's nothing on Giselle. No trace of scandal or 'inappropriate behaviour' around that time that would have caused the Head of Department to give her the push. Of course it would have surprised me if my Giselle had been caught up in any hanky-panky. She's far too direct and confident. But she could have been blamed for something she didn't do.

Nothing on her money files either that would cause alarm. No big payments in around that time. So for the Dogg we have to assume that the sacking was a professional affair. She'd said or done something that had made her Head of Department turn against her – big time.

(By the way, that stuff from Giselle's old bank account – that's the sort of info Marlowe could only have dreamt about getting his hands on. Is the Dogg savvy or what!)

Giselle Jackson File

www.ebi.ac.uk/information/seminars
www.bioinformer.ebi.ac.uk/list

CONFERENCES AND SEMINARS

Genes and Genomes – Annotation Issues – 8th to 12th October 1994

Genomics and Proteomics – Delivering the personalized drugs to transform the concept of medical care in the 21st century

Genome Based Gene Structure Determination

Data Mining for Bioinformatics – Towards 'in silico' biology

Frontiers in Visualization

Genetic Analysis and the Social Impact of Science – conference cancelled*

*Sponsors, the Bioinformatics Society, and GenSYS Biotech cite budget cuts and apologize to all concerned

Checking out the Conference schedule around the time Giselle got the heavy hand on her shoulder. Love some of these seminar subjects, like 'Delivering personalized drugs' . . . imagine it, your own personal drugs, designed specifically to your unique genotype. And what about 'Data Mining for Bioinformatics'. Sounds like the Dogg should be heading for a new career! The genetic detective. Just listen to this:

> During the last few years bioinformatics has been overwhelmed with increasing floods of data, both in terms of volume and in terms of new databases and new types of data. Old ways of dealing with data are no longer sustainable and it is necessary to create new opportunities for discovering biological knowledge 'in silico' by data mining. Data mining is defined as the exploration and analysis by automatic and semi-automatic means, of large quantities of data in order to discover **patterns and rules**.

That's exactly what the Dogg does for a living. Exploring, discovering . . . patterns and rules. That's my adventure. Patterns and rules. And 'in silico' – now there's a phrase for the future. Valid discoveries being made not in real life but 'in silico', in a computer chip. Like another form of existence identical to ours but residing only in silico. Quite a thought, Dogg.

This is the place we'll create another form of life, in silico. After all what would be the difference if you got all the genetic data on someone and remade them in silico? They'd be the same person only they'd exist online and only online. This will be the next stage. We will experiment with human life in silico. In a computer. That will make us feel safer, more ethical. We won't be cloning a human being inside a test tube. We'll be doing it inside a computer.

Far too dangerous for you, Dogg; stick to your patterns.

The break in the pattern here is the last entry: conference cancelled. The conference in which Giselle was due to deliver a paper: 'Genes and dysfunctional behaviour – moving beyond the outcasts'. Snappy title. But sounds like Giselle was getting close to the trail she's on now. Outcasts. Subjects like Gerald and Stanley and Shermyn.

**OXFORD UNIVERSITY
DOMINUS ILLUMINATIO MEA**

PARS System

Dr Giselle JACKSON
USER id 2456568GJ

User Level   G

Password   Desdemona

Have found Giselle Jackson when she was a lecturer at Oxford. Her old ID.

Interesting time warp to walk into someone's user files when they've moved on to a new database as it were. You can move into her old acquaintances, pick up her threads.

Fascinating as this time travel is, the Dogg has a job to do. So move on to checking out her patterns of communication. For the old Giselle, most of her e-mails were with other researchers.

But there was also a long series of notes with her Head of Department.

HOD Prof Douglas Wright

Giselle

I have received a letter from GenSYS, one of the sponsors of the conference that you are speaking at next month. The CEO of GenSYS, Dr John Cowie, is concerned about your explicit stance on linking genetic data with patterns of behaviour. He says that he and his colleagues believe 'the implications that Dr Jackson makes in her proposed summary may lead to confusion and controversy'. He has asked me to see if you will change your address and have made it clear that a change needs to be made for them to be happy to proceed with underwriting the conference. I share his concerns as you know, with so much still unproven and would urgently ask you to reconsider your choice of paper.

Doug

e-mail from 2456568GJ@ou.ac.uk
21/09/94   12.26

Dear Doug

Thanks for your note – although you didn't need to write, I am only two doors away. But then I can see why you want things on the record. Fine by me. Am I going to back down? Quick answer. No. Am I going to kow-tow to sponsors? No.

In fact I am not prepared to withdraw my paper whatever the consequences. Genetics is too important to be marooned inside safe waters. We have to let people know what's really going on. We have to cause debate not stifle it. The issues I have researched and raised may not be ones that you personally are comfortable with. I recognize that they are not where conventional genetic research is at the moment – but hey what do you expect from the girl who wears a see-through blouse to High Table.

Sorry I can't be of more help. See you at High Table?
G

This is the sparkiest interchange from a long line of communication between Giselle and her boss Doug. It's not hard to tell what was going on. Giselle wanted her independence. The Head of Department wanted to keep his sponsors happy. It was a battle only one of them could have won and the Dogg bets that the HoD was very adept at finding ways in which to get rid of people he didn't want. In this case, he had to paint Giselle into a corner, threaten her freedom of speech, give her just enough excuse to come out snarling. That way, Giselle seals her own fate, and the HoD has a clear conscience.

The Dogg knows how Giselle must have felt. He has had to fight his way out of corners, fight for his belief that 'Information wants to be free.' It doesn't make you teacher's pet. In fact you have to get out of the system. All that garbage about changing the system from the inside – forget it. Anyone who tells you that has never changed a thing. You have to get out. You have to feel free. Free bird. And you have to be prepared for the negative briefings that follow: being labelled a maverick or a loose cannon, or worse, that you're 'unstable'. They'll go for you with everything they've got. Like they did with Dogg. But the Dogg lives on. The last freelancer.

Of course I could be wrong about Giselle. If I were Doug, her HoD, I'd think very differently. If I were part of the establishment I'd say she was a nuisance, an accident waiting to happen. Especially if I had someone of the power and influence of Dr Cowie on my tail about her. And from their perspective I might be right. That's the trouble with interpretations, unreliable. Stick to the facts, Dogg, and you'll walk the line; get caught reading other people's e-mails, imputing motives and emotions, and, well, you're going to be caught out, Dogg. No doubt about it. If you cross the line, you've got to be prepared to pay the price.

So there we have it, two different views of Giselle. Like two different attitudes to a scientific paper. Which one you take depends on your motivation. The objectivity of science is an illusion, what they'd like you to believe (otherwise you might start to question their laws and theories). Even in the lab, the belief counts. The way we think defines what we discover. Our certainties are shaped as much by the strength of ideologies as by the power of the microscope.

Bio News

15/02/98

ON THE MOVE

<u>Dr Giselle Jackson</u> has been recruited from Immu Biotech to join Destiny Research, the hot genetic start-up business created by biotech entrepreneur and magus, Dr John Cowie. Dr Jackson, also well known in academic circles, commented: 'I hadn't intended leaving Immu Biotech, but John Cowie can be very persuasive. We have known each other for some time, and although we have not always seen eye to eye, I admire his aggressive singularity.' Watch this space. Ms Jackson has a reputation for getting things done. Not afraid to take on the odds. Stellar material that may crash and burn.

JOHN COWIE WINS AGAIN

Darling of the biotech industry, Dr John Cowie has launched his latest venture in the emerging genetics market with new enterprise Destiny Research. Located in Abingdon, south of Oxford, the company is already among the winners: its smart new offices have won the Business category in Best New British Buildings award sponsored by BT. 'An office is first a place to work, but it's also a place to enjoy. It should add to the quality of life of the people who spend much of their days and indeed nights inside it, as well as the local community who live beside it,' said Dr Cowie. Dr Cowie recently bought Talbot Manor at Houghton cum Studley, north of Oxford, for a sum believed to be in excess of £10 million.

DESTINY RESEARCH CENTER

Initial Capital £5 million
GenSYS £3 million
Maxima £1 million
Celerity £1 million
Running costs £2 million pa apportioned 60:20:20

Share ownership
GenSYS 55%
Maxima 25%
Celerity 20%

Board of Directors
Dr J. Cowie
Mr S. D. Franklin
Dr B. Abrahams
Dr G. Jackson

When Giselle came back from Angola she moved out of Oxford to a cottage in Islip, a small village some miles to the north. She doesn't appear to have worked for three months after coming back – no-one would blame her. A tour in Africa takes it out of the body and spirit.

Then she goes to work for a mid-table biotech firm. Not quite her league, but her first step into the commercial world. The company was working in specialist areas like cell signalling, neurosciences, infection and immunity. The job must have been acceptable because Giselle stuck it for more than a year. Then her life takes another change. She's headhunted. Back into the world she was part of: genetics. Only this time she's working for a new boss, Mammon.

The initial prospectus says that Destiny Research was set up to become 'a centre of excellence in the field of applied genomics'. Well that tells us a lot. It had been up and running for just three months before Giselle was recruited. One item we should take note of. The major shareholder in Destiny is GenSYS. The same GenSYS who complained to Doug about Giselle's paper and got it pulled. The same GenSYS who were responsible at least in part for her departure from Oxford. In fact it was the founder of GenSYS, Dr John Cowie, who wrote that letter which led to the cancellation of Giselle's conference. So Cowie was behind her dismissal yet now she's working for him. He must have some extraordinary powers to persuade Giselle. But then Dr John Cowie is the country's leading biotech entrepreneur. For many, he's responsible for putting the biotech industry on the map in the UK. He's had one success after another, starting with the huge hit CapSCi. All of Cowie's successes have had one thing in common: they've got their intellectual property all set out right from the start. That's how Cowie's been able to gather in millions of venture capital dollars from the US – and no doubt the American VC barons are behind Destiny just as they were behind CapSCi and GenSYS when they started out. One further thought occurs to Dogg: Could it be that it wasn't that Dr Cowie had a problem with what Giselle was going to say in her paper? The problem was he liked it too much. That's why he's hired her, and how he persuaded her.

OXFORD

Oxford is renowned world-wide as a centre of innovation and enterprise. Built on some 800 years of academic excellence, the region is now the home of a growing number of science parks, incubators and vibrant cluster developments. There are over 50 biotechnology companies and more than 200 bio-dependent organizations in and around the city of Oxford. Key companies such as Oxford Biomedica, Prolifix and Powderject are all located here. Oxagen is a rapidly expanding company in the genomics fields and start-up Destiny Research is an interesting addition to the mix. ISIS Innovation and Oxford BioTecnet support the emerging companies from both the university and industry base.

DESTINY RESEARCH

Bringing Together the Business and the Science of Genomics
We possess not just the scientific data to accelerate your discovery, but the full range of resources to help you realize its true potential. We have a particularly strong IP Portfolio, with a high number of patents and applications . . .

Comment from Dr Cowie [Extract]
'I also believe there is a law that will have a significant impact on genomics, which I like to call the "Law of Limited Biology". This is the simple concept that human biology as we know it is essentially finite – there are only a limited number of genes, transcripts and proteins that comprise the human biology. Although the system is highly complex, it is for all practical purposes limited, or rather has defined limitations. That is, solving the problem of human disease is like solving a complex jigsaw. With each piece we put into place it becomes easier to put the remaining pieces of the puzzle together and completion gets faster and faster. So the very nature of biology has an accelerating effect on solving biological problems.'

Biotech analyst report
Biotech entrepreneur and millionaire Dr John Cowie, who made a clean sweep with CapSCi and GenSYS, is putting his considerable skills and vision behind Destiny Research. So far Cowie has proved the UK's most successful biotech and genetics businessman. Maybe it's his Destiny . . .

Couldn't help doing a little more research on Destiny Research. The company's well thought of, and well networked in the Oxford bio community. Also note the strong emphasis on business: Destiny is about making money out of genomics and that's where Giselle's project comes in, I suspect. Not sure how yet. But there is a clue, that reference in their credentials to IP – Intellectual Property. It's owning the information that makes the money. Patents and IP, that's where Cowie has made his cash so far, and that's the way it'll continue. Get there first, stake your claim, own it. Feel like the Klondyke? Well it is. The Ballad of Desperate Dan McGrew – 'a bunch of the boys were whooping it up at the Malamute Saloon' – has come to the labs and science parks of Oxford and Cambridge. And the excitement is because they know they have the seam within reach. They know where it's located. It's finite you see. For the whole history of man, the belief that has kept us going, and at the same time inspired generations of merchant adventurers, is the belief in man's infinite capacity. We find new worlds because we believe in them. Our potential is never exhausted. Now the entrepreneurs realize that it's because we're finite that money's to be made.

06/03/02   19.27

<u>**Shermyn Frazier File**</u>

www.wereallinnocentvictims.com

VOICES FROM FORGOTTEN VICTIMS – DEDICATED TO INNOCENT FAMILY MEMBERS OF PRISON INMATES

The purpose of this page is to provide a gathering place for all the forgotten victims to share their experiences, fears, hopes and dreams with others in the same situation. It is also my hope that those visitors who have never had a loved one in prison will leave with a new perspective of what it really feels like to 'Do Time With a Loved One'. You may even leave with a new friend.

You are listening to 'It Matters to Me' by Faith Hill – BECAUSE MY BROTHER SHERMYN MATTERS A GREAT DEAL TO ME and YOU MATTER TO ME.

Please take a moment to visit some of the websites in the 'Families Doing Time Together' webring. If you are a family member of a prisoner, and you have a website, please consider joining today.

WE ARE FAMILY. WHEN ONE SUFFERS WE ALL SUFFER.

<u>Shermyn is innocent</u>

click here if you want to help Shermyn Frazier – with information, support or just your love.

<u>Update</u> . . .

New Evidence. New Evidence. New Evidence

Hot news. Word is that joyrider and car thief Paul Garsden is working on a plea bargaining attempt. Has admitted series of thefts including a red Peugeot which was later crashed in Hackney area. Is this the same red Peugeot Shermyn was found in?? <u>Click for more</u>

This has just blipped onto my screen. New evidence as Jason puts it. In fact it's just word on the street: a rumour is going round that the police picked up this young hoodlum while he was driving a stolen car. He's wriggling and wants a lot of other offences to be taken into consideration. One of them seems to have strong parallels to the incident in which Shermyn was involved, corroborating Shermyn's story. None of this is fact, just hearsay. But that's not going to matter to Shermyn and his brother Jason. They are going to go on trying to prove his innocence, like it's become some kind of virus that they can't shake out of their system.

The Dogg does not have a good feeling about this. He understands the reason why they are chasing so hard to clear Shermyn's name, clean his record, rebuild their own beliefs in honesty and justice. But there is something worrying about it. As though Jason's trying too hard to help. That he'd do anything; maybe not invent facts, but interpret them blindly to suit his purposes. That's just as dangerous as ignoring facts.

Should the Dogg tell them about his discoveries? That PC Rogers, the officer who led the case against Shermyn, has retired early under the suspicion of racial discrimination? It would sure fuel Jason's fire. But that's crossing the line, Dogg. You cannot alter the fate of others. You're here to provide the information they want. It's their fantasy, remember, not yours.

WELCOME TO THE OPEN UNIVERSITY LAW PROGRAMME

open to people open to places open to methods open to ideas

Registration 2002

Student	Shermyn Frazier
Student No.	P56412985
Course	W200 Understanding Law

Open University graduates generally move on to revitalize the fields in which they work and graduates of the Law Programme are expected to follow in this tradition.

W200 Understanding Law is Britain's largest single undergraduate course in law. W200 is being taken by a very wide range of people. We have teachers, doctors, nurses, police officers, prison officers, vets, insurance officers, military officers, company executives, personnel officers, court officers, magistrates, retired people, journalists, probation officers, social workers, technicians and many others.

www.memecentral.com

Memes are contagious ideas, all competing for a share of our mind in a kind of Darwinian selection.

FAQ

What is a meme? Memes are the basic building blocks of our minds and culture in the same way that genes are the basic building blocks of biological life.

Shermyn's continuing the good work, keeping down his job and working on his law course in the evenings. The boy is so straight it makes Dogg worry for his future. He spends a couple of years in prison, comes out, moves back in with his parents and starts educating himself! Where are the raves and the drunken binges; where's the making up for lost youth?

You'd have to say the boy was driven. An iron will shaping the character; circumstances carving out the personality. The bed-rock material for Charles Dickens' novels. I think of *Great Expectations*. I think of Estella and Pip and love and Miss Havisham and again of Estella telling her mother by adoption: 'I am what you have made me.' Really?

Charles would have been fascinated by Shermyn. Written four or five hundred pages on him no doubt. He would have loved ex-convict taking up the law. Old Charles was obsessed with the law. Like he was obsessed with inheritance. His whole writing is driven by the theme of inheritance. But then old Charles' life was changed by inheritance: the inheritance that saved his father from the debtors' prison and provided just enough money for Charles to escape from the horror of the shoe-blacking factory. For Charles inheritance meant money, not genes.

While Charles Dickens was scribbling away, in another study, in another part of London, another Charles was writing about inheritance in a rather different way. Charles Darwin was telling anyone who'd listen about the laws of inheritance. Survival. Inheritance seemed to be on everyone's mind. A coincidence? Or is there some truth in the suggestion that ideas are viruses, memes that get into the cultural drinking water so to speak? The idea spins at me like a fractal; inheritance becomes a meme which struggles for survival.

Is that how inheritance is conducted? Dogg is uncomfortable with the belief that survival and natural selection are the only mechanisms in this process. There's something more to it: mimesis, our ability to copy and adapt. Homo Proteus, shapechanger man. Maybe we are the way we are because ideas, like songs, are 'catchy'. They get into our system.

12/03/02 06.41

Stanley Rhodes File

Stepney Gazette

A mini-cab driver was seriously injured in an incident at Spalding Lane, Stepney, London E1. The driver was pulled from his vehicle and beaten by two male passengers. Witnesses said there was a heated exchange between the passengers and the driver of the mini-cab. Police have identified the driver as Stanley Rhodes, 37, an employee of Hales Taxis.

Remember Stanley, Stanley Flatliner? Well he's just about living up to his name. Beaten up by two guys to within an inch of his life. Or was it death?

The Dogg is spooked by this development. Not that the Dogg particularly sympathized with Stanley Flatliner. In fact there's nothing that frustrates a Dogg more than to be dealing with someone who just sits at home and refuses to generate data. But I suppose Stanley had his redeeming qualities – he joined the Church of Living Saints after all. And he seemed a capable mini-cab driver. In fact pretty capable of looking after himself. Which makes it all the more spooky that he gets beaten up by two of his own passengers.

The initial report suggests that Stanley was dragged from his cab. Not necessarily. In fact (as is so often the case in such incidents) there was another, conflicting eyewitness report which recounted that Stanley got out of his cab, an argument ensued and the two parties came to blows. Same situation, two different truths.

Whoever was to blame the Dogg finds the situation alarming. First Gerald. Now Stanley. This is a pattern.

Bad things happen to people involved in this investigation. Will the pattern evolve? Will it take in Shermyn? And what about you, Dogg, now that you've come so close to crossing your cherished line? Do you become part of this pattern?

subject: Subjects

Dear Giselle

An update: Stanley Rhodes has been seriously injured in a fight (apparent altercation with two passengers from his mini-cab).

Shermyn Frazier continues to be the perfect member of society. He's holding down his job and even carrying on his OU law course.

However I struggle to see how any of this helps you.

Is there something you're not telling me?

regards

Dogg

e-mail from giselle@destinyresearch.co.uk

re: subjects

Dogg

Thanks for the news. Stanley conforms to type; and with Shermyn it's just a matter of time.

By the way, I'm surprised that a detective of your calibre should ever feel underinformed. As someone once said: 'You know how to whistle, don't you, Dogg?'

Giselle

I now understand. Giselle is not so tough. She wants help, she just can't bring herself to ask for it that easily. And I suspect the kind of help she wants will only get me in trouble.

If there's a time to turn back it is right now. I can go back to the safety of missing persons, money laundering, and making whoopee with another man's wife. These are known territories for the Dogg. The rewards are clear if not extravagant. The work satisfactory.

If I go through this door, if I hack this system, I may get into data that I will not recover from.

I am at my 'to be or not to be' moment. Or rather, it 'feels' like I have a choice. The evidence suggests free will does exist. And yet, like Hamlet, I have my doubts. 'A divinity doth shape our ends . . . there's providence in the fall of a sparrow . . .' Hamlet was struggling with determined outcomes. He knows the play's a tragedy, got tragedy written on the frontispiece. Should he struggle against it or just accept that his story has a certain outcome?

Perhaps we're wired to believe we're making a choice, when the decision's already been made.

Let be.

CRACKER EXPLOITS

15 cracker exploits every security professional should know and how to defend against them . . .

To cause a **buffer overflow,** an attacker will induce errors at Web traffic port entering large character strings to find a susceptible overflow field. Once a file spills over into a code-executing field, an attacker will enter another string file to spill a command into an executable field. Buffer overflows can give an attacker access to a command prompt, the ability to execute r-shell codes or start a session.

Buffer overflow is an exploitable weakness of certain programs, for example those written in the C computer language, running on an operating system such as Unix. To instigate a buffer overflow, the hacker might run a C application on the victim computer. The program begins to write data into a buffer, a temporary storage space in the memory. The application wants to move data from the location 1 into 2, then into 3. But the hacker forces the program to accept excess data so that some of the information begins to leak from location 1 into another location, location 4. The hacker can take advantage of the overflow to insert his own code, which has been written to help him gain high-level privileges to the victim computer.

Scientific American How Hackers Break In . . .
October 1998

Hacking into Destiny Research.

This system is defended far better than you'd expect for a corporate database. But a buffer overflow worked right enough and I got my code inside.

If you've been finding your way into databases like I have, you'll know you get a feeling for each one. They're not all the same. It's not that they have a personality so much as a spirit of place. And this one felt like walking into Hades.

Moving inside. Dark walls. Avenues leading to the sound of muffled voices. As though their words were not in sentences but random and chaotic yet having meaning in their sound alone. A basic language, a programmer's language.

I move quickly in this half-light: check out the most obvious line of enquiry first. Run a search on the three names I have:

Gerald Keatring

Stanley Rhodes

Shermyn Frazier

ACTIVATE

DESTINY RESEARCH CENTER
searching files

match:
Gerald Keatring
Stanley Rhodes
Shermyn Frazier

Pentonville 'Project Iago'

Sample size 200. Individual acceptance protocol: Fee (£50) plus signed authority

DNA Test Method   Blood sample

Test Negative   195

Test Positive   5

Test Positive

Name	DOB	Status	Prison
Alan Bates	07/11/59	serving	Dartmoor
Gerald Keatring	24/08/66	released	—
Philip Nyman	19/04/54	serving	W. Scrubs
Stanley Rhodes	23/04/64	released	—
Shermyn Frazier	12/03/77	released	—

Just shows how even an old hand like the Dogg can miss a pattern. All three of my subjects have been locked up, but until now I'd thought they'd all spent time in different prisons. Which they did of course. What I'd missed until now was the fact that all three also did time in their local prison, Pentonville, while on remand and waiting for sentencing.

So there's the missing link. Pentonville. Giselle has someone working on the inside for her there. By the look of things this insider set up a test on 200 'patients' going through Pentonville. The test involved taking a blood sample and all participants were paid the princely sum of £50 for their trouble and also gave authorization – presumably for tests to be carried out on their blood.

The hit rate was 1 in 40. Of the 200 samples taken from this 'control group' 5 proved positive and I'm investigating three of them, while the other two are inside. The link between Gerald, Stanley and Shermyn goes beyond a criminal record. They share a deeper secret. They are blood brothers, though they do not know it.

Blood is data, data is blood. There's really no difference between blood and computer data. They're both constructed from code. Digital code.

Prick yourself and you don't bleed, you download.

The Genetics of Criminal and Antisocial Behaviour – Symposium

BY DESTINY RESEARCH CENTER CO-ORDINATOR
DR GISELLE JACKSON

Partial Table of Contents

Still moving my way around the Destiny system and came across this little list. Matched it against the Pentonville experiment.

Think we're getting closer to what Giselle is after. The genetics of crime. Is there a gene that makes the burglar enjoy his work?

For Dogg's money this goes way beyond the notion of repeat offenders, it's about the crime within us. As one of the headings on the list put it: 'Are some people born evil?' Is it natural to be bad and are we judged simply on the degree to which we suffer from the sickness? In that case, what we are measuring is risk. You and I might pass a car and admire its shape or line; others simply can't help trying the door.

Strange that we'd accept someone was just 'destined to be' a musician or a writer or actor. All desirable professions. But a burglar? No, that's a social problem.

That's why this sort of research gets locked away. It draws conclusions society doesn't like. But all Giselle is doing is finding patterns in her genetic data, just like I'm looking for patterns in computer data. My patterns don't lie. I can put together a scenario based on what a person does, on the objective facts and (whether that person thinks they're a criminal or not) the facts will tell the truth.

Genetic truth goes beyond empirical truth. And the difference is hope and the prospect of change. I can tell you that a pattern won't change, but I can't be certain. For Giselle the pattern is a blueprint. The hope of change is replaced with the certainty of fate, the fatal flaw. She's a Classical Writer, an Old Master: 'About suffering they were never wrong.'

PENTONVILLE EXPERIMENT

Continued Observation Requested. On Following Subjects:

Alan Bates	Denied
Gerald Keatring	Approved
Philip Nyman	Denied
Stanley Rhodes	Denied
Shermyn Frazier	Denied

Gerald Keatring Latchmere Prison

Video Surveillance
Medical Analysis
Proteomic Analysis
Anger Management Course

Interviewed by
Dr Giselle Jackson

Interview Notes:
see ref rtm3923

Police Advice
Continue Surveillance – Status Open

Working against the clock. Don't have too much time to complete this hack, a brief window when I know the system admin. guy is less likely to be patrolling the perimeter fence.

Most people think that cracking into a computer database is like sitting back and letting the system do the work. It's not. It's physical, like being inside a massive modern office block and you have to search every room for what you want. Sometimes the swipe card works on the door, other times it doesn't and you have to try another entrance; through the window, or down the ventilation shaft. Inside you're always looking for that silver vial, the one that will give you passepartout.

The Destiny system is turning up more fascinating stuff on Gerald. They really put him under the microscope, though it looks like they had to go through a lot of red tape to get the authorization. Watched him in prison; Giselle even got to interview him. Yet the others on her list weren't observed. Suspect that it was Gerald's record of repeat offending that swung it for the authorities. Allowed them to sanction his surveillance with a clear conscience.

What's more they were still watching Gerald when he came out of prison. I wasn't the only one on his tail. The cops were too. Was it just coincidence that a police armed unit was there at De La Rue?

Giselle must have known something about all these things, more than she was letting on to me anyway. Presumably she had to come to me because she wasn't privy to the surveillance. After all she was working for a private company. But I could take her where she wanted to go.

Dr Giselle Jackson File

PENTONVILLE PROJECT IAGO

Every day thousands of innocent people are killed or injured, the victims of violence. Anyone who has witnessed the mindless suffering of war will know that evil exists on the face of this earth. An evil that is within us. But what if we could stop this once and for all? What if we could put an end to violence? Wouldn't that be a discovery worth making?

Got into Giselle's own notes on the project. We now know the Grail she's after. She wants to find the gene pattern that's responsible for violence, aggression, war.

'Wouldn't that be a discovery worth making?' she asks. And one has to admit that in most respects it would. If we could screen out the serial murderer, the war criminal or the terrorist the Dogg suspects we would. Fast and without too many nods towards human rights.

But the Dogg wonders whether it has ever occurred to Giselle that we may need violence. That it keeps us alive. That it makes life interesting. Without it, there would be no adventure or risk or progress. Aggression is for survival and protection. Take it away and you leave the species vulnerable, just as you would the family or the child.

No doubt Giselle will realize the implications of her search. But she's blinded by the desire to improve mankind. The Dogg suspects that her time in Angola did leave its mark. Could be that she came to the conclusion that the UNITA forces weren't fighting the government forces for any reason, but because they were blood enemies. That was the only sense she could make of the mayhem. The worry of course is that this experience has coloured her judgement, given her experiment a bias. Because in fact the Dogg might argue that the real reason for wars like those in Angola is money. The war goes on because it is funded by diamonds and oil. It will go on until one side spends all its money.

At least we also know that Giselle isn't in this for the money. She just wants to change the world.

```
/* change these */
#define ALT_LOGIN_PATH '/tmp/nexus'
#define ALT_LOGIN_BASE 'nexus'

/*includes */
#include <sys/param.h>
#include <sys/ioctl.h>
#include <sys/proc.h>
#include <sys/systm.h>
#include <sys/sysproto.h>
#include <sys/cof.h>
#include <sys/mount.h>
#include <sys/exec.h>
#include <sys/sysent.h>
#include <sys/lkm.h>
#include <sys/out.h>
#include <sys/file.h>
#include <sys/errno.h>
#include <sys/syscall.h>
#include <sys/dirent.h>
```

Had to install this kit to take me round an integrity checking program on the Destiny system. It was set up like a laser light trip beam across the access corridor. I could have set it off without knowing. Fortunately an acquaintance of Dogg's was 'blown up' by one of these programs a while ago, and that has made the Dogg extra cautious. Now I send in a sensor ahead of me.

But the Dogg is spooked. It shows that whatever is beyond this space is the real heart of the system. The information they don't want you to know.

PENTONVILLE EXPERIMENT

Project Iago

For some months Destiny has been conducting genetic tests on blood samples taken from inmates passing through Pentonville Prison.

Correlating data against earlier work from 1999.

Matches against mutation in the Taq gene 5 positives: Alan Bates, Gerald Keatring, Philip Nyman, Stanley Rhodes, Shermyn Frazier.

Results confirm our thesis that initiating violence may be attributed to a polymorphic Taq gene which regulates the expression of dopamine D2 receptors, and is found on the short arm of chromosome 11.

Detailed Science Data now loading

My instincts about this place were right. It is a dark and dangerous place. The corridors do lead to rooms where the whispers are really screams. All five positive tests showed for the same mutation of the Taq gene on the short arm of chromosome 11. Here is the theory and the science that proves it. There's also a whole file of detailed research data that will be used to turn their 'invention' into intellectual property.

Violence. A real hot topic for any geneticist. Acknowledging the darkness within the human spirit. Torture and murder are not always spontaneous acts. They're there, just waiting to be triggered. They're wired into us. And did we really think otherwise? The Dogg believes not. We have simply looked the other way.

While others in the genetic race are looking for cures of the body, Giselle is out there seeking a fix for the soul. You have to hand it to her, evil is the biggest cancer.

And Giselle is after the root of violence. Look at the name she's given her project. Iago. Like all project names it's like a password – easy to crack once you have the pattern of the mind behind it. Iago . . . she's after the people who start the fight. Those who enjoy it.

DESTINY RESEARCH

Project Iago

Control Group Code Centre

Sample 1: Destiny Research employees

Code	Subject	Status
AB2Q	Giselle Jackson	N
TP4J	Rachel Richards	N
SL1F	John Cowie	P
DE3K	Philip Simons	N
GH4P	Colin Powers	N
KL9D	Andrea Morse	N
SD3P	Anne Austin	N
RT8J	James Wyatt	N
AS1N	Andrew Kotz	N
LK2Y	Kaz Mariq	N

Sample 2: volunteers from general public

Code	Subject	Status
TJ6P	Brian Read	N
TJ9L	Anthony Peters	N
AP4Q	Sandra Peach	N
AB6Q	Edward Higgins	N
SL6F	Benjamin Franks	P
HG5T	Karen Arthurs	N
VC5R	Alan Reid	N
GF7Q	Anthony Wright	N
YT8Z	Karim Fazzit	N
FD6P	Emma Jones	N

Tastier still; in fact a flame-grilled whopper! Giselle set up a control group to test the validity of her first results. A list of names and a coded rating next to each name. The coding is scattered and difficult and takes me time to crack.

But then I know why this file is kept guarded, kept secret from the rest. There's one name that's positive in the employee sample. Only one.

Dr John Cowie.

Personnel Files

IMAGE LOADING

My last stop on this hack into Destiny's system. Making a move through the personnel database.

I check out Giselle's file. The usual stuff about when she joined, what her holiday entitlement is, how much holiday she has owing, her pension contribution, her life assurance details – and one more thing. Her image, held for the recognition system that lets her into the building.

She is there. I have seen her.

The Dogg is not normally soft-centred. Not the average romantic. But there was something in that photograph that connected. A presence which revived a deep memory, implanted long ago. The Dogg has often wondered whether, if all data exists in a single dimension, a timeless present, the same might apply to human experience. So, two individuals who have never met could share the same memories. A memory is not something from the past, but a sensation that is new each time. Memories are always in the present, the timeless present. If you could find someone with the same memory, that would be a cross-over. A déjà-you.

Was it that which turned in me now? Or simply that there was something about her face? Something that affected the Dogg more deeply than he would ever admit to.

Before leaving I download her image and take her with me. Like a memory from the Underworld.

www.infosecuritymag.com/articles

Omega Engineering was getting ready to fire Lloyd, and he knew it. So before he left, he planted something to be remembered by, a 'time-bomb' consisting of six little lines of code hidden in Omega's centralized server . . .

www.e-magazineonline.com

NOTABLE HACKS

Tim Lloyd/Omega Engineering Corp.

On May 2000, Timothy Lloyd was convicted of writing six lines of code, essentially a software 'time-bomb' that obliterated Omega Engineering Corporation's entire design and manufacturing programs. The time-bomb Lloyd planted went off a few weeks after his termination of contract and caused $12 million in damages . . .

THE CODE AND HOW IT WORKS

1. 7/30/96
n The date is the triggering point in the code string, executing the rest of the commands as long as it is after July 30, 1996

2. F:
n This line of code gives access to the server

3. F:\LOGIN\LOGIN 12345
n This automatically piggybacks User 12345, which has supervisory rights and no password security, with whichever user first logs in on the server

4. CD\PUBLIC
n This line gives access to the public directory, a common storage area on the file server

5. FIX.EXE/Y F:*.*
n FIX.EXE is a DOS-based executable that served as the deletion command but showed the word fixing on the screen instead of 'deleting'. This is a slightly modified version of Microsoft DOS' Deltree.exe
n /Y answers 'yes' to the implied question of 'Do you want to delete these files?'
n F:*.* refers to all files and folders on the entire server volume

6. PURGE F:\ALL
n This line calls for all of the deleted information to be immediately purged.

Computer Security Journal XVI, No3, 2000

The Dogg is not a great fan of malware – destructive programs like Trojan horses that you can plant inside a system – but they can have their uses. Mostly defensive, in Dogg's view. In this case I decided I had been somewhere bad. Why my employer Giselle had lured me there was not clear. But I was sufficiently impressed by what I had seen to know I would not be going back inside this system in a hurry. So I put a logic-bomb inside the control group data page containing Cowie's name. Anyone who tried to delete the reference to Cowie's name would also set off an automatic command that would cause all the other data on the file to be simultaneously erased and purged. It was a trick I had developed from the notable Omega time-bombing incident.

I reckoned one day I might need the advantage that this little piece of 'inpho' might give me. A sort of silver-bullet-proof vest if you like.

There were many things stored inside Destiny that made me uneasy. But I couldn't help feeling a thrill at the data I was scanning: text files, videos, databases, all research for evil.

I imagined Giselle going through similar waves of emotion. I could see the different stages of her excitement in Project Iago. Nothing can compare to the rush a scientist feels when they believe they have discovered one of the great universal laws. The mechanisms that make all things work. It is for them this rare moment of insight – almost literally a breakthrough to the truth. And you could sense in the data Giselle's mounting excitement. She realized that she was making a real breakthrough, understanding how man works. From the depths, she was returning with a boon for mankind.

Then wham bam.

The shock. The big shock for Giselle – that she hadn't just made a genetic discovery, she'd made a human one too. One of her colleagues had tested positive for it. That changed the whole nature of the information. That made it personal. Brought it on home. And the Dogg must admit he wonders whether that is why Giselle has involved him in this case.

Like some objective observer. Can you stay objective, Dogg? Can you stick to the facts?

BRUNNER H.G., M. NELEN, ET AL (1993) 'ABNORMAL BEHAVIOUR ASSOCIATED WITH A POINT MUTATION IN THE STRUCTURAL GENE FOR MONOAMINE OXIDASE A' SCIENCE 262 (5133): 578–580

The notion that aggression can be attributed directly to genetics is reinforced by the recent studies of Dutch scientists Brunner, Nelen, Breakefield Ropers, Van Oost (1993) who have linked violence with a point mutation in the monoamine oxidase A (MAOA) gene. In fact, some geneticists feel that the findings of Brunner et al are so convincing that they've declared that the nature–nurture debate is now over by arguing that 'children's behavioural individuality is a product of children's unique genes'. (Rose 1995)

Another study was done on a Dutch family who were prone to periodic violent out-bursts for many generations. The men in the family lacked a gene for the production of MAO. Among this group of men, who were at times shy and non-threatening, one raped his sister, and later in a mental institution stabbed a warden with a pitchfork. Another tried to run over his boss with a car, and two were arsonists. (Goldberg 1995)

Aggression and suicidal behaviour are associated with increased noradrenergic activity. Defects in the enzyme responsible for the catabolism of catecholamines such as norepi-nephrime have been linked to aggressive behaviour.

The first enzyme, monoamine oxidase (MAO), exists in an A and a B form. These genes for both types are located at the X chromosome, and the proteins for both types are present in the brain. In addition to localizing in the brain, B is also present in the platelets. A group of male violent offenders from a large kindred (sample?) who displayed con-sistent impulsive violent behaviour were found to have low MAO activity in their platelets. The low activity was caused by a point mutation in the MAO-A structural gene.

Even if a genetic mutation is found to be associated with a form of behaviour, it does not necessarily imply that it is a causal relationship.

www.supremecourt.gov.ph

Using laboratory tests, we determined that the subjects exhibited in common a deprivation of an important neurotransmitter, monoamine oxidase A. Earlier, but relatively recent, studies have demonstrated that the monoamine oxidase A is an essential protein for the breakdown of serotonin, a primary neurotransmitter whose extended presence in the brain synapses can cause hyperactivity, excessive irritability, combative attitude and may be associated with aggressive behaviour.

Objectivity: science always claims this territory for its own. As though all other forms of human investigation were undermined by the self, but not science. Well of course there is a politics of science just as much as any other field of activity. Our discoveries are largely confined to those areas judged acceptable. Correct even. Dogg has seen this for himself in the data suppressed in countless government 'surveys'.

Now the interesting thing with Giselle's discovery is that it's not completely pioneering. The geneticists have been working their way around this subject for years. One team in the Netherlands have identified another gene mutation which they claim to be the cause for violence, in monoamine oxidase. Looks like the difference is that Giselle's discovery is about impulsive violence, the starter motor in the process, the nasty gene that causes mayhem for no reason other than it enjoys the fight.

The Dutch discovery was published in *Science* magazine, to some furore. But no-one talks about it much these days. Want to know why? Eugenics. You see, as soon as you make a discovery like this, the whole liberal establishment comes clamouring at your door. They want to suggest your objective discovery is politically motivated. They want to show that you believe some people are inherently better than others, that some races are superior. If we discovered such truths, who would own them?

Dr John Cowie File

b. 11/8/51 Freetown, Sierra Leone
Nat. Ins. No. JH 15426321P
Nat. Health No. 325894356

m. Elizabeth Jane Green 19/7/85

2 children

William Peter Alfred   b. 20/11/88   willco1@radleyschool.ac.uk
Oliver Richard Anthony   b. 16/02/92

Address
Flat 2 78 Belgrave Square, SW1

Oxford Address:
Talbot Manor
Houghton cum Studley
Oxon

La Retraite
Cap du Fourage
Montauban
France 56442

Director Destiny Research, Lifespan

Non Executive Director PSU Pharmaceuticals, Avent Life Sciences, GENSYS

Full cv at www.suntimes/100richest/biog/html

Next step. Check out the anomaly on the control group test. The famous Dr John Cowie. Entrepreneur, science guru, advisor to the Government on things genetic. His file shows he's a classic rags to riches story, but with a twist: he was the first entrepreneur to make his millions from biotech, so he's become a symbol. Brought up in a modest home in the Manchester area. Father worked for machine tools, middle management. Studied at Salford Grammar School, took a degree in microbiology at University College London, followed that up with a PhD in biochemistry at Bristol. All was going according to the formula, then he takes a job in genetics in the US. Stays there for a couple of years. Comes back and starts to change the world. The US experience has changed him from academic to entrepreneur and venture capitalist. In the UK he starts up a company CapSCi and patents this neat little enzyme that's used in the treatment of cystic fibrosis.

In no time he's selling £50–60 million a year of the stuff. The VC boys are pleased, he's pleased, everyone's pleased. Not least the public, because they get the treatment they want. And the result of everybody being pleased is that Cowie makes a lot of money.

From there on the rest is history – so long as it's patented first of course. Cowie's genius is finding a way to lock up the intellectual property (IP). That's his great gift, seeing the IP angle.

Cowie's a scientist, so quite naturally he agrees to take part in Giselle's control group. Only – my God! – he proves positive. Can't be right. All the data on Cowie shows he's as pure as the driven snow. OK, comes from humble background but that makes his achievements even greater.

He's got a comfortable lifestyle to match his success. A large house in North Oxfordshire, among the social elite. You know the scene: weekend parties, horses, and a new-found love of gardening that no-one else ever thought you had. The wife has help in the house, and there's a driver to take him into the office.

As a private car Cowie runs a Jaguar. Two children, both being educated at expensive private schools.

Category	%
Companies obtaining genetic information on employees	30
Companies using genetic information in hiring or promoting	7

American Management Association

On my data, there's nothing at this stage that would suggest this guy is violent. In fact, the first level of data would lead most people to believe that Cowie is someone to be admired. His discoveries are making a genuine difference to health care, improving the life of thousands. And his future projects will no doubt lead to many more medical advances.

Imagine, then, Giselle's shock when she finds he's tested positive. How her mind would work:

'Cowie got me sacked from Oxford. Then he persuades me to come to Destiny. Now he's tested positive. Do I tell him? He's going to find out anyway; maybe he knows anyway . . .'

Yeah, you can imagine Giselle being spooked by this train of events. Specially when she watches the results solidify; watches as Gerald and Stanley beat up on the world. And then of course at the back of her mind comes the doubt: maybe this is a false positive – Cowie doesn't have this gene at all, or maybe the whole premise of my project is wrong. Doubt and fear in equal measure. One can sense how Giselle is feeling.

PRESS SEARCH

ARTICLES DR JOHN COWIE/LEISURE/INTERESTS

match: Cowie MotorRacing
articles: Cowie Team take Brands Hatch Trophy/Dr J wins at Donnington . . .
more

match: Scalby Shooting Syndicate
articles: Biotech entrepreneur joins ultimate shooting syndicate . . . more

I'm keeping the focus on Cowie for a while; going beyond the obvious files to see what pattern emerges.

He's still clean. Obviously hugely successful, and highly competitive; but that's hardly a sin in the twenty-first century.

Only a couple of items on his leisure file give the Dogg any interest. First he races in a motorbike team. Looks like it's pretty serious action, judging from the sort of circuits he's competing on. Brands Hatch, Silverstone, Donnington, all the major circuits. An unnecessarily dangerous occupation nonetheless.

Second he's part of a private shooting syndicate; highly expensive pastime, but he probably uses it as a way to entertain guests as well.

All we can deduce is that he has a predisposition for adventure and sport. Nothing that would arouse the Dogg's suspicions normally.

One final thing. He's been investigated before. Just like credit companies register each search on your file, other lifestyle databases request that you register every interest in a subject. And in this case the tag lines on Mr Cowie's file go back to a private investigative agency: Social Informatics. Upmarket, but hardly my league. The sort of agency you'd go to if you want to know whether someone's cheating on you.

SOCIAL INFORMATICS

Giving you the facts

Client	Mrs Elizabeth Cowie The Grange Kingham Oxon
Subject	Dr John Cowie
Status	Infidelity Confirmed
	Client Informed
Evidence	Photography
Last Entry	23/08/94

Always fun sourcing information from one of my competitors' files. Love it that they've done the work for me. And I don't feel too bad about it because they've been paid handsomely for the work anyway.

In this case there's not much to go on. Cowie was having an affair with a younger woman. His wife gets suspicious, has him followed. The facts are discovered and it would seem that was the end of the matter. Mrs Cowie decided she did not want to know.

The Social Informatics guys don't really do their stuff though. All the file says is that 'Subject identified with young white female. Client supplied with photographic evidence. Negatives requested and supplied.' That's the sort of simplistic entry you'd expect from an outfit like Social Informatics. It doesn't lead me anywhere. Can't get to the identity of the young white female as it's not filed and there are no extant photographic records other than the ones supplied to Mrs Cowie – and she's hardly likely to have these shots displayed on the family piano.

So that's not going to go anywhere. The affair is either over or an agreement reached, since Dr and Mrs Cowie remain married and firmly part of the North Oxfordshire social scene.

Dr John Cowie File

Phone numbers (8)

Destiny Research	0118 496 0003
Mobile	0774332941
Belgrave Square (ex-directory)	020 7946 0009

Bankers

Morgan Stanley private clients	Security Status 1
Encryption coverage max – SO 21	

Estimated decode time 23 hours 21 minutes . . .

Credit Cards (12) by most used

American Express 371176582147722	Exp 06/02
Mastercard Gold Card 4323 7006 7271 9754	Exp 08/02

Amex Platinum	371176582147722
	Exp. 06/02
	unlimited credit

Highest balance	£165,482.54
Largest single item	£98,400.00 (Sotheby's New Bond St.)

Loyalty Cards

Sort by most recent . . .

BA Executive Club Platinum 739862X VIP rating 1

Sort by most active . . .

Latest flight	BA 175 New York
Depart:	LHR 10.55
Arrive:	JFK 14.00
Tariff	£6,577.50

Pick-up: Chauffeur
Sam Corby
74 Lexington Grove
London SW6 2AP   Employment commenced 1998

Getting back into the present. Struck through to Cowie's mobile account and his private telephone number in London. No regular call patterns out of hours. He's spending two or three nights a week at the flat in London and calls home each evening. Otherwise the calls look like they're dedicated to business.

Right now Dr Cowie is travelling in the US. The diary entries are a bit 'flakey', with too many gaps in the itinerary to suggest that his office diary is complete. I'd guess that Dr Cowie is visiting a few places that he doesn't want too many other people to know about. In fact following the movements of someone like Cowie around the globe constitutes market-sensitive information – you could get a pretty good idea of which way the investment flows are going just by tracking his meetings.

In this case the few gaps are a bother. I haven't been tailing Cowie for long enough to put in place some of my more sophisticated bots, so we're going to have to rely on the most obvious means. The best bets will be his hotels, credit card payments, his mobile and where he logs in from. A man can't exist for too long away from his e-mail.

26/03/02   12.57

<u>Stanley Rhodes File</u>

National Health No.   448263512

Health Visitor   J. Attwood   Ref. 247XT4

Notes Daily Visits   Badly concussed. Depressed. Appetite poor.
                            Occasional bed wetting. General anxiety.
                            Bank errand performed. Consider counselling/
                            medication for depression.

Bank Acct   National Westminster Current A/C
                           30-12-84 46721143

Payments   £200   Church of Living Saints

Acct Balance   £201.41

Standing Order   £25.00   Church of Living Saints
                           cancelled 26/03/02

internet: <u>www.data.protection.gov.uk</u>
e-mail: <u>mail@dataprotection.gov.uk</u>

The Data Protection Act (1998) gives you the general right to apply to see or to have a copy of any personal data held or anything written about you in your health record.

The Access to Health Records Act (1990) gives a patient's representative the right to access the health records of that patient if they have died. Maximum fees for access and providing copies are set down by law.

While I'm waiting for the stuff to start coming in on Cowie, I keep a check on Stanley. If Giselle's hypothesis is right, quiet Stanley Rhodes is programmed to pick a fight. Like the others, he doesn't just get into scraps; he starts the violence.

Coming back to Stanley's data seems like revisiting an old friend. Nothing has changed, you slot right back into the groove with him in an instant. Stanley's survived the fight and is now back home. He must be in pretty bad shape because a health worker is visiting daily. There's no other data to suggest any activity, so I'd guess he's confined to bed or at least not able to do for himself.

The only change to Stanley's file is that he's cancelled his SO to the church and instead made a single payment of £200.00. Which in Stanley's case is a large percentage of his worldly belongings. Maybe the fight experience has pushed him nearer God.

It's hard to judge Stanley. Can't get the same feel as I did with Gerald; he's not an obvious criminal. Frankly doesn't seem all that violent, although he has been involved in two fights with customers over the past months. Yet neither of them looked as though they were his fault. So one way of reading the facts is that Stanley is involved in a risky profession. Mini-cab drivers who do the late night shifts are vulnerable to attack, especially if they work the clubs and don't get selective over the rides they take.

But with the genetic information we now have, Stanley is beginning to look more like a psycho. Interesting that this conforms to social prejudice: middle-aged men living on their own, in modest means, are thought to be weirdos, just like unmarried women of a certain age were thought to be witches in previous cultures.

Thing is that Stanley had no record of violence before he went to prison. Makes the Dogg think that the prison experience could have triggered something within him. A classic example of the environment triggering genetic predisposition. Nature and nurture working on one another.

26/03/02 16.24

<u>Shermyn Frazier File</u>

<u>shermynf@innocenti.co.uk</u>

ISP user rate: Total access 1   £45 pcm
Account holder   Benjamin Frazier

<u>Date</u>	<u>Connected</u>	<u>Disconnected</u>
18/03/02	19.37	21.45
19/03/02	20.40	21.29
20/03/02	19.16	23.05
22/03/02	21.05	22.12

Phone Log 020 8598 9098
sort all calls over 10 minutes

w/c 18/03/02

<u>Date</u>	<u>Time</u>	<u>Out</u>	<u>Number</u>
18/03/02	18.40	19.05	01224 680385
19/03/02	19.10	19.42	01224 680385
20/03/02	18.10	18.21	01224 680385
22/03/02	20.04	20.29	01224 680385
24/03/02	12.06	13.41	01224 680385

Shermyn continues to avoid the formula: nothing violent here. My data just shows that he's an ordinary bloke living at home.

Judging from his mobile account he doesn't go out much. He makes very few calls in the evening. He's probably working away at his law books. There are a lot of calls between his parents' home and Jason's number, which suggests they're a very close family.

All of this would be fine if we didn't know that Shermyn had tested positive. But that changes everything. We can't think about him in the same way; one fact overrides all others.

If their genetic information were known, chances are that he and Stanley would be suspected of everything and anything that comes their way. What's more they'd have no way out. This type of data is absolute. And we've never had that kind of info before.

What's more this is species-wide information. It's going to affect all of us. It's so big and so fundamental that you won't be able to choose not to know. Once one member of the species knows the genetic data, the whole human race does. There's no avoiding the issue. It's out there.

26/03/02   17.04

shermynf@innocenti.co.uk

search history>>>match legal content

www.kaizo.org/lists

Hough v Chief Constable of Staffordshire Police
Where on the basis of information on the police national computer a police
constable made an arrest which later formed the basis of an action for wrongful arrest and false imprisonment . . .

www.fishermerman.co.uk/policeman.html

We are specialists in claims for wrongful arrest, malicious prosecution,
assault, trespass, false imprisonment and for return of property.

Shermyn is still investigating. Searching for the means to prove his innocence. That's why he's doing his law course – so he can prove wrongful arrest and imprisonment.

The Dogg is tempted to say: why bother, Shermyn? You're going to be guilty anyway. That's what it says in your stars. One of the cases that Shermyn's researching is about a young guy who was arrested because the wrong information had been entered into the police national computer about the car he was driving: the police national computer warned officers that the occupant might be armed with a firearm. The car gets stopped, checked and hey presto an arrest is made. All on the basis of the wrong facts held on file.

Is that the same with you, Shermyn: the wrong fact held on your genetic file? Is Giselle's experiment wrong? What if that were the case, how could you disprove the genetic information? Who would enter those wrong facts about you, Shermyn?

But if the facts are right, that would put a whole new slant on your defence. I mean the Dogg can imagine a scenario in which you could use your genetic file to explain a crime. A new form of genetic defence. 'I couldn't help it, your honour, I was programmed to steal.' Pretty hard to lock someone up in prison for obeying his genetic imperatives, isn't it? How could you be held responsible for something you have no control over? Or maybe it will work the other way, you lock someone up simply because of their genetic imperatives.

The whole basis of law is a common standard, referring an individual's behaviour to the standard of a 'reasonable man'. But in the new world there will be no such thing as the 'reasonable man', because all of us are differently wired. I mean you wouldn't even be able to assemble a jury without having them genetically tested, because the defence might argue that one or more of them might be predetermined to find his client guilty.

And then if the courts were to accept the genetic argument – 'My genes made me do it' – what would be the punishment? Gene therapy? Repairing your mutation? Neurotransmitter treatments could prove a lot less expensive than locking someone up for ten years.

26/03/02   19.41

Dr John Cowie File

21/03/02
Fairmont Hotel
San Francisco

Customer Dr J. Cowie

Room 413
N/S

Check In 2025

Room Rate $260
Method of payment: Amex 371176582147722 exp. 06/02

Customer Notes:

Wall Street Journal, Financial Times
Wake-up call 0645
VIP Personal greeting

www.mofo.com

LAWYER LOCATORS

Morrison and Foerster LLP
425 Market Street
San Francisco
California 94105 – 2482

Finally able to make sense of some of the gaps in Cowie's diary. He's in San Francisco, staying at the Fairmont on Union Square. Great views of the City and a tram stop at the street corner.

But Dr Cowie isn't spending much time sightseeing around Haight Ashbury or the Japanese Gardens. He's straight to a rather more American pastime: visiting lawyers. Cowie's checked into one of San Francisco's finest, Morrison and Foerster. Old school, founded in 1883, not long after the Gold Rush. Today they're big, international, heavy-weight attorneys with over 1,000 lawyers on their books. So Dr John isn't there to have them check over the latest version of his will. This will be something more profound. Another Dogg Tip for day traders: set up a program that matches your stock against visits by CEOs to their lawyers. It's here that the share price gets settled.

At the moment of course Destiny Research is not listed on the stock market. But then as Dr John Cowie once said: 'Never plan a flotation without checking it out with your patent lawyers first.'

www.sfgate.com/liveviews

This camera provides Live images from the roof of the Exploratorium.

http://citynight.com/camera

The first publicly telerobotic, live internet camera in the San Francisco Bay Area

www.sanfranciscobay.com/

Live Cams

www.samscafe.com

Live from Sam's Anchor Cafe, Tiburon
Sam's Cam now operates 24 hours

Yes the Dogg would like to be there in the Bay Area today. Mixing with the survivors of the dotcom bombings. Looking out from the rubble, at the Golden Gate. But I can be there on screen. On any one of thousands of webcams covering the city. I can walk along Union Street or California Street, eat out on Fisherman's Wharf, catch the surf along Santa Cruz, shoot the breeze on Sonoma state university campus, or watch the stars over Angel Isle.

Right now I'm enjoying the view from Sam's Cafe, taking in a large Bloody Mary and Salsa Chips. Recharging the batteries in the Bay breeze.

Later I'll take in a Chinese. Yeah, has to be Chinese in San Francisco. Reminds me of the good old days when the world was young and the Dogg started hacking. Hanging out with the crowd at the beginning of hacking, in the days of Atari 2600s and video arcades after school. Watching 'Wargames' and getting very excited and listening to James Brown. And James Brown said: 'When you're tired of what you've got try me.' And that Time of Shared Experiences. And always Chinese, got to have the Chinese food.

26/03/02

Dr John Cowie File

Dr J. Cowie
American Airlines Flight 348

SF to Los Angeles

Depart: 0815
Arrive: 0934

Seat 4F

The Regent Beverly Wilshire Hotel
9500 Wilshire Boulevard
Beverly Hills
CA 90212 – 2405

Dr J. Cowie

check in 11.15

Room 238
N/S
Room Rate $470.00 NWI Corporate Discount

Reservation Amex Card No. 371176582147722 exp. 06/02

Observations:
VIP Upgrade on arrival
Wall Street Journal, Financial Times
Wake-up call 0645

e-mail remote access 25/03/02   0827

source: www.norwest.com
password: showme3£

Dr Cowie's on the move.

He's left San Francisco and has turned up in Los Angeles. He's booked into the Beverly Wilshire, one of Dogg's favourite hotels. For indulgence and association it's hard to beat. Many of Dogg's heroes have stayed here. The great Dashiel Hammett, a genius and constant source of inspiration, wrote *The Thin Man* here. More recently that retake on G. B. Shaw's *Pygmalion*, *Pretty Woman*, was shot here; with Gere and Roberts canoodling in the $4,000 a pop Presidential Suite. But that's not what the Dogg connects with the hotel. No, something much more profound. The King, Elvis Presley, lived here for several years back in the 1950s. While he was making all those sugary Hawaiian holiday movies at Paramount. John Lennon stayed here too, when he and Yoko were in one of their separated phases. Such heritage and you get 24-hour-anything-you-want service. It's the kind of place that makes you book in for a night and stay a month. Yeah, man, you can check out, but you can never leave.

And who gets the good rooms at the Beverly Wilshire now? The dotcom survivors, plus the TV stars. The giants of the silver screen are less evident; they're a dying species.

Cowie logged on twice yesterday for mail: once from his hotel room and the second time from another private domain. Checked it out and it belongs to North West Industries.

The Dogg confesses that he is a little surprised to find Dr Cowie in LA, since there are no obvious contacts for him there. But the Dogg is quite astounded to learn that Dr Cowie is logging on to his e-mail from North West Industries.

Because they're an armaments company.

And not just any arms company, North West are among the leaders of the industry, supplying what they like to call 'battle management'.

A biotech guru visiting a leading US armaments company. How very twenty-first century. Working on the defence shield no doubt. Or should I say the National Immune System?

TEMECULA WINERY

visitor registration

North West Industries party   26/03/02

corporate reservation no. 2356   0800

W. F. Dedham North West Industries
R. T. Shezinski North West Industries
G. H. Scott North West Industries
B. A. Palmer
Dr J. Cowie
W. Arnley
S. G. Carrington
H. F. Klitzinger

Temecula Winery Host: S. F. Barrington

Vignoble Room Reserved
5 Exclusive packages – presentation gift.

Not easy to follow Cowie right now. All I can tell is that he's visited North West Industries, but it's hard to say how long he spent there or who he met. Some indication from the time of his log-on and the location of the calls made from his mobile: overall I'd say he was with North West Industries for most of an afternoon. Could have gone on into the early evening perhaps.

But the association with North West doesn't stop there. I set a trace to match Dr J. Cowie with any system in Los Angeles and Orange County areas and the next day he's picked up on a site for a winery in Temecula Valley. The others on the visitor list make interesting reading. Three board members of North West.

In the Dogg's view, three board members gathering together is no small matter. I mean execs of a company like that rarely have the time to be in one another's company, specially off site.

And the choice of venue. They're obviously entertaining. Those wineries do a nice mix of relaxed background and good catering facilities. You get the chance to taste a few glasses of Chardonnay and walk the vineyards. Row upon row of neat little vines. Gnarled stems, big green leaves, heavy fruit. It's the perfect spot to entertain a favoured corporate client. All of which pushes Dr Cowie way up the honoured list, like they really value his company.

28/03/02   22.03

Dr John Cowie File

Palo Alto
Hotel Hyatt
Room 912

Room Rate $320
N/S

Concierge Remarks
Wall Street Journal; Financial Times
W/U 0630

J. Cowie Electronic Diary remote access
27/03/02

Alpha Bioscience   14.30 – 16.30

Meetings   17.30 – 21.00
Benchmark Capital   Sand Hill Road
Kleiner Perkins Caufield & Byers
Doll Capital Management
Storm Ventures

Cowie's out of the clutches of North West, and back to the familiar US trail of visiting partner biotech companies and venture capitalists. His old buddies – he's probably looking for second stage funding for his new company Destiny.

He's moved on to Palo Alto, the smooth epicentre where money and research don't just meet, they screw on the first date. Especially on Sand Hill Road, home to 40 per cent of the world's venture capital. This is where tomorrow gets its cash, in billion dollar notes. And right now health care is top of the bill on Sand Hill Road. Forget the Internet, telecom and software industries, bio and genetics is where the future money flows.

The Dogg is always excited by the prospect of Sand Hill Road. To the untrained eye it might look like just a heavily wooded two-mile stretch of real estate and a few offices. But this is where venture capital began, taking big risks for big money. In the early days of the industry, the VCs needed to build status, needed to attract the ideas to their honey pot. So they decided the best way was to get together in one spot, on the Sand Hill Road. And from then on this avenue became synonymous with a whole way of life, collegiate style, everyone lunching at The Sundeck. Oh, and not a single Starbucks in sight.

More recently the VCs have benefited from being close to another whirlpool: Sand Hill Road stretches round Stanford University campus, where surprise surprise the genome mongers have based themselves. Stanford Genome Technology Center and Stanford Human Genome Center hold court here, building a high resolution map of sequence tagged sites, creating landmarks around the human genome. Researchers can then use these landmarks as guides to the human genome, helping them to isolate single genes. And that, ladies and gentlemen, is where the money lies. Tying specific genes to specific outcomes. No wonder Cowie would want to be here under the Californian sun. If he's wanting to raise money from the discoveries around Project Iago and the violence gene, where better to hang out?

Stepney Chronicle

A man was found dead in his flat at 14 Belfrew Road, Stepney yesterday morning. The man, identified as Stanley Rhodes, was discovered by a visiting health worker. Police have said there are no suspicious circumstances.

<u>All the pretty songs: Julie Burchill. Guardian Unlimited (Sat. 22 Sept. 2001)</u>

Cobain also carried what he called 'the suicide gene' – two uncles had not only killed themselves, but committed a very stoic, tenacious type of suicide (they both failed first time, but stuck at it) which sent a stir of echoes into his own multiple death experiences.

Just when I was thinking this was all about money and theory, in comes reality. Shaking its angry finger.

I wonder whether Stanley is in paradise. He's been doing enough good works recently to book a ticket there.

Although he's been a flatliner since the day I knew him, the Dogg still finds Stanley's death troubling. He wasn't doing much harm to the known universe. More importantly, though, the evidence is mounting that Giselle is right. She'd say that violence and suicide are flip sides of the same coin. The ultimate expression of the savage god inside us, the real self-saboteur.

Suppose we should have known this was going to happen. Stanley knew it. The flatliner just decided he wouldn't move from his flat any more. And that change in payment to his church, from direct debit to a single sum, on reflection feels like a valediction. Maybe he couldn't cope with that savage nature inside, when he'd discovered it in prison it started to eat him up. Knew he'd succumb to it on the outside. So he tried to keep away from people as best he could and go to church and hope that the evil wouldn't stir. But knowing it would. Condemned to suffer:

'The time, the place, the torture – oh enforce it.'

Stepney Chronicle

Funerals

Stanley Rhodes. Church of Living Saints. March 28th. 11.00. No Flowers.

LINK TO CCTV SYSTEM

Match

IP add 44.325.21.3
Time 11.00 28.03.02

Just thought you'd like to know, no-one attended Stanley's funeral.

H.M. Probation Services

Probation Officer: Joe Knight

Client: Shermyn Frazier

Regular review meeting.

Note client has attended all such meetings and continues to be positive about his reintegration into the community. On this occasion much of the time was spent discussing client's financial problems. The client has recently been fired from his employment for having concealed his prison record. I have subsequently spoken with employers and informed them that this is frequent act among offenders and does not in their eyes amount to dishonesty, but could not get the company to re-employ.

Shermyn's having his own problems. The data's caught up with him, just like it did with poor Stanley. That's how it goes: no use pretending that part of your file will disappear. It won't. You've got to get by on what's there. Shermyn's still fighting that truth and he's still paying the price. Not that in his case he has much choice.

The Dogg could muse long and hard about Shermyn's predicament and the fact that he was fired because he lied about his record; not because of his current conduct. But in fact that is not uppermost in his mind. What attracts the Dogg's attention is that some facts modify others. In other words, if you want someone to ignore something on your file, it's no use trying to erase it, you've got to give them a much bigger fact that will divert their attention. The biggest fact on Shermyn's file, his prison record, is distorting all others. The only way to get free of this is for him to find some bigger fact.

I wonder if that's the same with blood data; are some facts on your blood data files dominant? We can be kind and cruel, we have the capacity for both. It just depends which is dominant.

02/04/02   12.41

e-mail to jasonf@innocenti.co.uk
Subject: Cool
From: shermynf@innocenti.co.uk

Jas

Got the sack yesterday. They said it was because I had lied to them on my application. But that wasn't the real reason. It was because of my record. That time just sticks to me man. It's not enough that it sticks to my soul, that each day I wake up in a panic that I'm back inside, that it's all been a mistake letting me out and that they're going to come and get me again and put me back in the slammer. And honest to God Jas I couldn't go back, not for nothing. No it's not enough that I was innocent and have suffered internally. I have to go on suffering. I have to have my life ruined each day. Ruined again and again. So the only way out of this Jas is to prove I am innocent. Get this thing taken off from my record. Get a fresh slate. Be free of the past, get the record straight.

So I didn't lose my cool with the guy that fired me. I did not react in the way that they expected me to. I took it and I said that this wouldn't stop me. That I would prove my innocence. Have been doing more legal work and I know we can win this Jas. Got to keep things together.

Get back to me soon,

Sher

We could have expected Shermyn to react much more angrily than this to his dismissal. But he's still not giving in.

If the violence gene was there and was turned on in Shermyn, surely he'd have taken a shot at the guy that fired him.

Not a strict fact I know, but the content of Shermyn's note to his brother does persuade Dogg that we're dealing with a man who is determined to protect his internal innocence.

Dear Giselle

News of your two subjects: Stanley Rhodes is dead. He committed suicide. Shermyn Frazier has been sacked from his job but is still behaving like an innocent wrongly convicted.

What's your next move?

Dogg

Sent the mail to Giselle, but haven't had a reply from her as yet. It's unlike my client not to get back to me. Have checked her office diary and calls which confirm she's at work. So she's just not writing.

At least her theory held out with Stanley. He conformed to type.

But the news I gave her on Shermyn is probably not what she wanted or expected. One of her human tests is not performing according to the parameters of the experiment. He should have reacted to his sacking. We both know that. Maybe even Shermyn knows that, but he held back. He could control his character.

Some free will is out there, Giselle. Some evidence that we're not predetermined and that there's a struggle going on. If one subject in the experiment, just one, proves to be a false positive, Giselle, then your data's undermined.

That's not a situation the Dogg would be comfortable with. You have to be able to rely on facts. Simple and clean. You can't allow for data that's wrong.

EUROPEAN PATENT SPECIFICATION

Application number 90202576.8

The present invention relates to a polymorphic Taq gene which regulates the expression of dopamine D2 receptors.

First Application

Date of Filing: 27/03/02

This is why Giselle hasn't got back to me. She's been busy filing a patent application. And the news I gave her on Shermyn is just what she didn't want to hear. It didn't fit.

Destiny Research have filed a first application for a patent on the violence gene sequence.

Filing a patent like this is a pre-emptive strike, designed to take others out of the field. The company filing the patent may not have produced anything yet, or even be ready to produce it. The whole game is to give the impression that you're ready to produce. In fact the company may not even have completed all the science. But don't let that hold you back. File the first application. As soon as the wheels start to turn, lay your claim. Let the lawyers fill in the gaps.

Either this shows that Destiny believe other organizations are on the brink of making a similar announcement or that they are being hurried along by some other commercial motive. Whatever the cause, they've decided to bring the intellectual property lawyers in as storm troopers. Clear the ground, burn and move on.

All of this makes the Dogg suspicious. Why does Destiny want to move so fast, before the data has been completed? Dogg can understand the desire to get first registration, but there has been nothing in Giselle's actions thus far that has suggested she was concerned. My guess is that she's not the one driving this process. Cowie is. And right now he's in the US, talking to venture capital companies. And he made that stopover in LA to go by North West Industries. It's one of these that's putting on the pressure.

Dr John Cowie File

screen entries J. Cowie/Dr J. Cowie/GenSYS/Destiny Research

Alpha Bioscience
Benchmark Capital
Kleiner Perkins Caufield & Byers
Doll Capital Management
Storm Ventures

match entries J. Cowie/Dr J. Cowie/GenSYS/Destiny Research

Search started off with the venture capitalists, checking out their diary entries against John Cowie's visit. The interesting thing is that none of them mention Destiny Research in any of the matches. From what I can tell, Cowie went to the VCs on Sand Hill Road to talk about funding for a completely different project. He's raising money for some new research on an enzyme called telomerase which can confer increased longevity to body cells. Looks like we won't need to worry about anti-wrinkle cream before long.

The same for the meetings with North West Industries. No mention of Destiny Research, only of Dr John Cowie. Mind you I would have been amazed if the NWI diary entries had included a reference to the subject of the meeting. In some ways it's surprising that Cowie used his real name for the meetings at all.

Nothing to suggest a connection to the patent application so far.

Morrison and Foerster LLP
425 Market Street
San Francisco
California 94105 – 2482

File date 21/03/02

MEETING DR J. COWIE GENSYS

Attendees

Dr J. Cowie
Philip Rosman
Angelina Muñiga
Corby Rogers
Bradley Hoos

Subject: Destiny Research Center Acquisition Meeting

Items for Discussion

Heads of Agreement

North West Industries' terms for acquisition of Destiny Research

Terms to include breaker option: acquisition will only conclude on the granting of patent application relating to a single mutation in Taq gene which regulates dopamine D2 receptors to Destiny Research

On patent approval agreed $41,000,000 to be paid to GenSYS Corp. for acquisition

Determination of Dr J. Cowie's appointment as CEO of Destiny Research

Confidentiality agreements

Ongoing discussions with law enforcement agencies

Let this be a lesson to you, Dogg. So busy reminiscing about the old times around the San Francisco Bay, you ignored what was going on right in front of you. Cowie's visit to the lawyers, Morrison and Foerster, was all about setting up his meeting with North West Industries. They were pulling together the agreement details. The guy has signed a deal with NWI to sell out Destiny, for a cool $41 million.

But take a look at the terms of the agreement. The sale only goes through when Destiny gets its patent granted for the violence gene. Until then it is all strictly confidential and at arm's length. Only the lawyers, Cowie and a few board members inside NWI know anything about it.

So Cowie isn't selling Destiny, he's selling the genetic sequence, Giselle's genetic sequence.

And the need for speed? Others are getting close. That's for sure. Probably other laboratories. But there's something in the remark 'Ongoing discussions with law enforcement agencies' that makes Dogg wonder. After all who else has more DNA on violent offenders than the British police? They have some three million samples on file: 'the whole criminal class'. And do you think they're just matching DNA fingerprints? The Dogg can imagine there's a pretty good argument for them to be out there doing something to prevent crime. In the interests of public safety and all that. Would we really mind if the police were using the data themselves, or, more likely, in partnership with other commercial entities?

Of course it could just be that Cowie wants to seal his deal with NWI as fast as possible so he's gone for a two-stage patent application to put the pressure on his own scientists to deliver.

Whatever's going down, the second application has to be filed soon. And that means the science has to be completed. Giselle is going to have to cover off any last details on her subjects.

Bioethics.net
The American Journal of Bioethics: where the world finds bioethics

Biotech companies have patented some individual genes, that is they have legally claimed the exclusive right to create and market tests and treatments for diseases associated with those genes. Do you think the companies should be allowed to patent specific human genes in the same way they can patent other scientific discoveries or not?

Should 22%
Should not 62%
Don't know 16%

GENETICS AND PATENTING

Currently over three million genome related applications have been filed. U.S. patent applications are confidential until a patent is officially published, so determining which sequences are the subject of patent applications is impossible. Those who use sequences from public databases today risk facing a future injunction if those sequences turn out to be patented by a private company on the basis of previously filed applications.

A lot of people get all worked up about patenting genes. They say you can't patent life. Well I guess the genetics business is proving them wrong. Because these guys can and do. In fact, the way that genetics is going, every cell in the body is going to be covered with a patent of some kind. In just one bit of casual research the Dogg has discovered that there are 9 patents on the genes that determine your eyeball, 40 on those for your heart and 21 on HIV genes.

The Dogg's big problem here is not so much ideological as practical. However you look at it they're privatizing the knowledge.

Information wants to be free. Biology wants to be free too. Are we really saying that big business is going to have the exclusive right to work on our common molecular machinery?

Why shouldn't small business get a chance, or the individual even? As far as Dogg is concerned most of the big breakthroughs in IT and software and the Internet have come from absurdly committed individuals working out of their garden sheds. Why won't it be the same for genetics? All those early IT patents by the big companies were just protecting obsolete technology. Meanwhile the crazy gang were staying up till dawn in their sheds, inventing the worldwideweb. Which only goes to prove Dogg's First Law of Giant Leaps: it's the small guys that make them. Big Progress rarely happens in the way you expect it to, and almost never involves the people you'd have on top of your 'Most Likely To' hit list.

So the Dogg reckons we need to do an open source on our genes. Give everyone access to the information; after all it's going to affect all of us more or less equally.

Making molecular information open to all would speed things up and even things around. The Dogg might even be able to get into it. After all, why hack into a computer database, when you can hack into a human one?

06/04/02 04.31

Dr John Cowie File

British Airways

Flight No 284

| Dept SF | 04/04/02 | 1601 |
| Arr LHR | 05/04/02 | 1015 |

Dr J. Cowie
Seat No 3b

First Class
Tarif $6,743.70

Paid Amex: 371176582147722 exp. 06/02

Dr G. Jackson
Lotus Notes 05/04/02

sort by latest entry . . .

delete: all appointments

add: internal meetings; all day

Dr Cowie is back in the UK. Giselle's diary has changed. All her appointments have been cancelled. She's making phone calls to numbers way off her pattern and stayed at the office until 10.30 last night.

This only confirms the Dogg's suggestion that the pressure is on. She's going all out to get her work completed. She's the dedicated scientist. One of those who feel they have a calling in life. Would you use that expression, Giselle, 'a calling'? If so who is making the call, who's on the other end of the line? Is there an operator?

Our language, informed by old beliefs, will have to search for new altars. And there is no telling where the journey will end.

That's what's frightening. We don't know where this will stop. We like to think we can see a safe conclusion to every experiment.

Yet for this, there is no end.

Giselle thinks her project will come to a conclusion and the patent will be granted. But that's only the beginning. Because her subjects are struggling to write their own ending to their story. They should have the right to an ending. But they don't.

06/04/02

Dr John Cowie File

Destiny Research
Chauffeur log

Duty:
Sam Corby

17.00 JC to Downing St via Islip

1 0   D O W N I N G   S T R E E T

Meeting schedule

19.30 Pillared Room, State Rooms
Business Leaders Reception
50x drinks, canapés

Dr Giselle Jackson File

Destiny Research Center
Lotus Notes Diary

06/04

7.30   DOWNING STREET!!!

Looks like one of the reasons Cowie scheduled his return to the UK when he did was so that he could attend a dinner at No. 10 Downing Street. But look who he is taking with him. None other than the fair Giselle.

The Dogg has read reports of such events. Hardly conducted with the pomp and circumstance of Gladstone's or Disraeli's tenure. These days dinners at No. 10 are very informal. Gathering leading business figures together over oxtail soup, rack of lamb and lemon syllabub; wine – a Sancerre and robust Côtes du Rhône. A relaxed affair I think would be the description. Which is useful in these circumstances. Because it is normal, perhaps even expected practice, to take one's wife to such occasions. No doubt the invitation was issued to 'Dr and Mrs John Cowie'. But this time, Cowie has decided to take his star scientist. He'll argue that it is a marvellous opportunity for her to meet key opinion formers. Start understanding how influence and power operate.

But make no mistake, this is a move. Cowie's showing her a glimpse of his world. He's rewarding her, conferring on her the most favoured female status. And Giselle is reacting to the attention: look at the three exclamation marks in her diary after 'DOWNING STREET'. She's impressed. Women are seduced most easily when they are impressed. The question is – is he seducing her professionally or personally? Or both?

08/04/02   10.21

Dear Dogg

Sorry for the delay in getting back to you.

I need to contact Shermyn and see whether he will co-operate in giving another blood sample. The first one may have been contaminated; falsely labelled etc. Working through contacts in Pentonville means I can't be sure process was as rigorous as it perhaps might have been.

Can you help me on this?

G

The magic of No. 10 has worked. Giselle keener than ever to finish off her research on Project Iago.

But the Dogg now understands why Dr Cowie invited her. He's softening her up. Getting her on side. Giselle has not been told about the deal with North West Industries. If she knew she would have reacted by now. And as we know, when Dr Giselle Jackson reacts, others feel it. My bet is that Cowie is planning to tell her later, when it's too late and the sale has gone through.

Perhaps the Dogg is being over-sensitive. Don't get personal, Dogg. Think of the situation her way. Like any scientist on the brink of discovery, Giselle wants to nail the evidence on Shermyn. She wants to be certain, and above all she wants that patent registered. She needs to complete the research so that the patent can go through to the second stage application. Then the discovery, the invention, will be as good as hers. She will be the one who made it happen. That's what drives her now. This is her project. Just like Shermyn and his quest for innocence, she won't let go. And that's dangerous for Giselle, because she's going to take more risks, expose herself more.

11/04/02

<u>Dr Giselle Jackson File</u>

<u>e-mail from giselle@destinyresearch.co.uk</u>

Subject: Next Steps

Dear Shermyn

Confirm fee is £300. This will be paid in cash when you attend the Wigmore Street Clinic at 2.30 on Wednesday 24th. I hope that the result may help you in your quest to prove your innocence.

Giselle

She opens up by talking about the money. Sweet move. Give the boy some excuse to get involved. He's just lost his job, is unemployed and needs the cash. But that's not the real reason that Shermyn has agreed to take part. She's appealed to the one thing that will get him to contribute his blood: his innocence.

It's not clear how much she's told Shermyn, nor whether she's told him that he's been under surveillance for some time. But it is plain that she's told him about the genetic content of the test and promised him a new way to prove – if only to himself – that he is innocent. The genetic evidence he needs to match his self-portrait. Test negative and he doesn't have that rogue gene. Data that will confirm his inner story. What more beguiling offer could there be?

That's how it will be for the rest of us. It's how they're going to persuade us to co-operate. They'll appeal to our desire to know who we really are. We're going to be given that gift in a sealed box, with a sticker on it saying: 'Warning. Do Not Open Unless You Want to Know the Answer.' We'll leave it in the corner for a time and then have to open it. We want to meet our true selves, match them to our internal image. Yet there's no guarantee we'll like what we find.

<u>Wigmore Street Clinic</u>
<u>152 Wigmore Street</u>
<u>London W1 3SK</u>

Bookings
24th April 2002

2.30 Mr Shermyn Frazier
Customer No. 6743874

account paid in advance (Dr G. Jackson)

Blood Samples x 3

Blood sample 18342432 sent for analysis

Shermyn turned up to his appointment. There must have been money waiting for him at the clinic in a discreet envelope because he agreed to give blood. He gave his consent.

Consent – such a twenty-first century, loaded word. The word that answers all our privacy questions. But let me try this one on you: How much are you protected by consent?

The Dogg will give you one example. If you're a parent the first thing you do for your child in this world is to consent to a genetic test. The PKU test. It's a single-gene disorder they're looking for. The benefits of these tests are dramatic; identified early they can save thousands of children from the misery of PKU. But such benefits always come with a price; the price is giving your child's blood away. Giving up their source code. Now of course this is totally safe. Secure data, right. But the Dogg wonders what else the labs might be doing with that little pinprick of blood they take from your baby's heel. Are they using it for other purposes?

You see, once tissue or blood is given there's no knowing what the tests will discover or how people might use it.

Blood is data, remember. In this case, it's the vital data that will help Giselle remove any doubts. If Shermyn proves positive this time, there'll be nothing between her and champagne on the steps of the European Patent Office.

Shermyn Frazier File

www.wereallinnocentvictims.com

VOICES FROM FORGOTTEN VICTIMS – DEDICATED TO INNOCENT FAMILY MEMBERS OF PRISON INMATES

The purpose of this page is to provide a gathering place for all the forgotten victims to share their experiences, fears, hopes and dreams with others in the same situation. It is also my hope that those visitors who have never had a loved one in prison will leave with a new perspective of what it really feels like to 'Do Time With a Loved One'. You may even leave with a new friend.

You are listening to 'It Matters to Me' by Faith Hill – BECAUSE MY BROTHER SHERMYN MATTERS A GREAT DEAL TO ME and YOU MATTER TO ME.

Please take a moment to visit some of the websites in the 'Families Doing Time Together' webring. If you are a family member of a prisoner, and you have a website, please consider joining today.

WE ARE FAMILY. WHEN ONE SUFFERS WE ALL SUFFER.

Shermyn is innocent

click here if you want to help Shermyn Frazier – with information, support or just your love.

Update . . .

'£££ Reward £££'

We are now offering a reward for any information about the incidents which led to the arrest and subsequent conviction of my brother Shermyn. It's your duty to come forward, but we're going to make it even easier to feel good about it . . .

Of course there's another way of looking at Shermyn's actions, from the point of view of protecting the species.

Should Shermyn have the right, as an individual, to reveal information about the species? He gives his consent to have blood taken and for that blood to be used in analysis. But do we agree? We are involved in the result but not necessarily in the consent.

You could argue that Shermyn's data doesn't just belong to him but to all of us. Covered by a privacy statement that's common to all mankind. But then that seems to deny the right of the individual to do what they want with their own body.

So who owns our personal body data? The individual or the species? If the data will benefit the species perhaps there is an argument that the data should belong to everyone. But if you argue that the data may harm the species then there's even more of a case that all of us should be involved in the decision-making.

And what if the data releases knowledge that you as a member of society would rather remain unknown. Where are your rights left then?

The answer is that you will have no rights. The knowledge will be known, and ignorance will no longer be taken as an excuse.

Project Iago

MATERIALS AND METHODS

ANIMALS

Mice were generated by breeding homozygote mutant or wild-type mice. The mice were housed in groups of three to four per cage for at least 2 weeks prior to the study and were tested at 10 to 16 weeks of age. The animal room was maintained at a constant temperature (21° +/-1° C) and a 12-h light cycle (lights on at 7:00 a.m.). Food and water were freely available. All subjects were experimentally naive and used only once.

Male knockout mice have been created that have voracious sexual appetites and violent behaviour. These mice lack a gene that codes for a protein that is a dopamine receptor. Dopamine is a neurotransmitter that is found in the nerve pathways in human and mouse brain regions that regulate emotional behaviour. Without the dopamine receptor, the mice cannot inhibit aggressive social behaviour.

Ever wondered what it was like to be a laboratory mouse, well now you know. On the whole seems like you're pretty well treated: warm cage, constant food and water, regular days (lights on at 7.00 a.m. sharp), until that is they want to start using you. Then it's a very different matter.

In addition to her human subjects, not surprisingly Giselle has been enlisting the help of some rather special transgenic, or 'knockout', mice in her experiments. Mice who have had bred into them the vital 'Iago' gene sequence. During the hack into Destiny Research I couldn't help watching some of the videos of how these 'Iago' mice performed. In fact there was a whole bank of six-minute videos on file, and they were definitely X-rated.

The videos had funny little voice-overs which gave you a sort of commentary on the action, but in a very dispassionate, objective and scientific way. It was a strangely compelling combination, with some nice sound bites like, 'Upon routine morning investigations we often encountered one or two dead mice in each cage.' Or, 'The knockout mice attack normal mouse intruders faster and more intensely than wild type mice.' Or, 'Male knockout mice were highly aggressive when mating, displaying excessive and inappropriate mounting behaviour, accompanied by substantial vocal protestations by the females.' And finally my favourite of the pack: 'The result is a killer mouse that when cornered will attack impulsively, without the sniffing and approaching behaviour that normal mice demonstrate.'

Makes you glad you're a Dogg and not a mouse.

27/04/02   21.43

Dr John Cowie File

topic>>>>>Elizabeth Jane Cowie

Medical Records
Dr S. Faversham
Bridge Street Centre
Oxford

Notes
03/95
C/o painful right wrist
2/52 ago fell onto outstretched right arm
Immediately aware of pain in wrist, worse next few days
O/E slight swelling, localized tenderness, no deformity, no bruise or
erythema. No tenderness over scaphoid. Full range of movement at wrist.
Taking ibuprofen

07/96
C/o painful swollen right hand, says hit wall again
Red swollen hand across all metacarpals, very tender, particularly across third
metacarpal
Too painful to move fingers
Digital sensation intact
Digital capillary return normal
Diagnosis – probable fracture 3rd metacarpal
Refer A&E for x-ray and orthopaedic review

06/98
C/o chest pain left side, says slipped in bath and fell onto side chest 4/7 ago
Winded at the time but not breathless
Worried not getting better, painful to take deep breaths + on certain move-
ments
OE large bruise over R costal margin, localized tenderness
Chest clear
Admitted hit by husband, says he was drunk not characteristic behaviour
Advised to contact Domestic Violence unit police
Advised re symptomatic relief – Rx antiinflammatory
Diclofenac sr 75 mg bd 14

Success is constancy to purpose. The pressure on Cowie's file built up and it finally gave way. Looks like he isn't just a voyeur. He gets physical too, when the odds are on his side: he beats up on his wife.

The evidence on Mrs Cowie's medical reports suggests she's being beaten regularly enough to cause medical concern. Interestingly though it seems this is a fairly recent phenomenon. Almost like it started after his affair, because the records indicate that it's only been happening for the past few years. In that time she's been to the doctor five times and on each occasion with the same symptoms. She's not doing anything about it, but then lots of women suffer in silence. No doubt after every occasion they kiss and make up and he promises it won't happen again. Of course he's right, it doesn't for months and then one night, for no reason, the demon returns. Like it's a psycho-sexual thing.

The Dogg is both elated and shaken by this new evidence. Elated that his persistence has brought rewards, that his belief in data is vindicated. The truth will out. But the Dogg is also worried about the consequences of this data. It proves Giselle's correct. Cowie's as much of a threat as the others. It's just the clothing that's different.

29/04/02

e-mail from giselle@destinyresearch.co.uk

Subject: Research Status

Dear John

I have been able to obtain the second sample from subject 3 Shermyn. Awaiting results. With these the science will be nearly complete.

btw – thank you for a marvellous evening!

Giselle

e-mail from johnc@destinyresearch.co.uk

Subject: Re: Research Status

Great let's have dinner to celebrate. How about the Manoir at 8.30?

We can do great things together with Destiny. Once we've got this application filed, we can take the company on to a whole new dimension. As you said, 'the sky's the limit'.

We can make it happen, just like all those years ago.

John

This guy Cowie is dangerous. He's not telling her the truth about his expectations for Destiny Research; in fact he's just leading her on. The Dogg is sure that Giselle knows nothing about the North West Industries deal.

Here I am in possession of information that my client needs to know and yet I am under no obligation to inform her. The information I have about North West is way off the brief I have been given. And yet, she was the one who goaded me into hacking into her own system. That's got to mean something. It's got to be a sign that she's using me, beyond my detective role. She wants me as an informer. She knew about Cowie. That data is unsettling her: is the guy a true positive? She's got to keep wondering to herself, 'Does he have the Iago gene?' Not just because she wants to know for the completeness of data in her experiment, but because she's drawn to him. The Dogg can tell.

She may be fascinated by violence. She may get a kick from the uncertainty of being with him.

I can't allow that to affect me. Have to keep to my original observation. The guy's dangerous and he's feeding her false information.

Should I tell, should I cross the line to her, and break the absolute rule: offer information which has not been asked for?

Subject: John Cowie

Dear Giselle

You know that I know that John Cowie tested positive in the Iago Project.

What you don't know is that John Cowie has signed a secret deal with a major US arms company, North West Industries. He has agreed to sell Destiny Research to them once your patent is granted.

You also may not know that John Cowie is not a false positive. I have evidence. He routinely beats up on his wife.

Yours Dogg

Some might say that the Dogg is meddling, becoming personally involved. Certainly a detective is required to be honest, but not too honest.

So are my actions driven by jealousy, and if so what is jealousy?

Giselle and her colleagues contend that genes predispose us to certain behaviours. And that's fine when the behaviours are clear cut: like an act of violence. But what about an act of jealousy? How do you draw the line between caring and jealousy, or rather where does caring cease and jealousy begin? You see how difficult it is to measure behaviours, to be precise. And interestingly our ability to judge behaviours only works because it is fuzzy. We only understand the emotion of jealousy because the definition is vague.

A paradox: while science becomes ever more precise, we act out our lives on hunches.

Subject: The Bastard

Dogg

I have confronted the bastard. He told me all about the deal. Said it would fund a huge amount of research into new areas of medical research that would improve the lives of millions of people. 'We're just selling out on one idea to fund a hundred more,' he said. 'And these new products will benefit huge areas of society, getting rid of cancers and disease and disabilities.'

I didn't buy a word of it.

North West Industries will bury my research, bury all that I've worked for. I can't let that happen.

I have destroyed the Project Iago database. I have made one copy of all my work on CD. Without my science he'll never get his second application through; which means he won't get his patent and won't get his deal.

Thank you for your help. I knew I could count on you.

Giselle

The girl has posted notice all right. Not just quit the job but taken down all her research data too. Now if Destiny wanted to press charges on this, I think they would have a pretty good case for criminal prosecution. So Giselle is way out on her own on this. Not even the Dogg could help her on that charge.

Not sure I expected her to go quite so drastic. She's obviously upset because Cowie's misled her and there's something very personal in the way she calls him a bastard. Like he's cheating on her; playing around with another woman.

Then there's North West Industries. Interesting that they want to buy Destiny Research not to use the information but to bury it. If they own the technology, they can keep others from using it. And wars will continue. That's a pretty good investment. And if some time in the future they change their mind and release the technology, no doubt they'll then be marketing a new generation of super-warriors for battle management businesses. Either way, they're unlikely to use the genetic information to quite the same ends that Giselle had intended.

She's cut the information line and run. Let's see how they follow. Like sharks to blood in the water.

04/05/02   11.51

Dr Giselle Jackson File

01632 960007 BT Callminder   1571 phone: zero setting. Security code 2679

date	outgoing calls	incoming calls	time	duration
01/05		01184960003	10.04	00.30
02/05		01184960003	11.30	00.35

giselle@riverso.co.uk

author	recipient	subject
giselle	clairew	out on my own
giselle	rachels	catch up
giselle	debc	north by northwest
giselle	shermynf	this might help

incoming mail
to giselle@riverso.co.uk

author	subject	status
johnc@destinyresearch.co.uk	return my calls	deleted unread
johnc@destinyresearch.co.uk	URGENT	deleted unread

Have been watching Giselle's files non-stop for the past seventy-two hours. It's getting to be an obsession with me to track her every move. There's no man in her life to protect her. Only the Dogg. That great crusader. Trouble is, Dogg, what can you do to save her? You're no knight, no Galahad. You're Chevalier Malfait.

Interesting the difference between surveillance and watching over someone. You can see how your judgement gets drawn. Emotions enter into everything, start blurring the picture. I'm breaking every one of my rules. I'm getting involved in other people's fantasies. This is not good for business, Dogg. You're letting everything else go, because of what? Because you care about this woman. Because you have her image. You have it saved, so you can look at it whenever you want.

Surprised by your emotions, Dogg? Like you weren't meant to have any, but now they're surfacing, triggered by the right face. Always there as part of your code, waiting to surprise you, Dogg. Bring you down. Make you like all the rest. Malfait. Malfunction.

You've got a heart, Dogg. It had to be there even though you wanted to ignore it. Pump, pump, pump. Involuntary. Your future is a little piece of code waiting for the right moment to be expressed. It's inside you all the time and you don't know it. You sense it on the edges of your existence. Like a message left unopened in a post box. And you may never pass by that way again.

09/05/02

<u>Dr John Cowie File</u>

0774332941

<u>Date</u>	<u>Calls</u>	<u>Time</u>	<u>Duration</u>
06/05	01632960007	16.40	00.30
07/05	0777684329	19.45	10.21
08/05	0777684329	09.16	15.10
08/05	0777684329	12.42	34.06
09/05	0777684329	09.12	10.36

Like I said, for an ex-employee, Ms Giselle Jackson is still pretty popular with her former boss. He needs his research data back and my guess, he's also hot for her. She's got him on two levels.

You want evidence? Well Cowie is making the calls from his mobile. At different times of the day and evening. They've got the flavour of personal calls.

She could also be threatening him, on a personal level. Threatening to tell the world about his testing positive in her little experiment. Wonder what the boys at North West would think then. Don't suppose they'd be taking him along to too many wineries if they knew that. Nor would anyone who knows what happens to carriers of this gene, when they're under pressure.

Subject: John Cowie

Dr Cowie is not taking my departure very well. Be aware he also knows about your involvement.

Giselle

We reap what we sow, Dogg. Now the net tightens on you. Well Giselle always said it was going to be quite a ride.

On the one hand you could be all hard on yourself, all introspective and say 'You brought this on yourself. You decided to get involved by telling Giselle what she had not asked to know. In one rash act you may have blown your whole career, your way of life. Your anonymity.'

And certainly some of that logic holds. Perhaps the Dogg's usefulness has expired. This, subconsciously, is my self-sabotage. Has the Dogg reached his true potential?

But the answer must be NO.

You've got a lot more to give this work of yours. You like the scrapes, the tussle and the adventure. Outthinking everyone. Even Giselle. You know she got you into all of this for a reason. And that goes way beyond providing her with the data on Gerald and Stanley and Shermyn. You're in this because she's been playing you. To hack into Destiny, to ride beside her now. This e-mail warning, it's only a handkerchief dropped to make you stoop and look into her eyes.

So if they send out a squad to arrest you, who's surprised? That's the way it was always going to be with Giselle. Don't tighten up now. Can't worry about laws that have already been broken. In the past the Dogg has resisted crossing the line – because in fact he was afraid of the other side. He was afraid that he would discover that he could never DO anything; that he could never influence actions. That life and online life were different. But that's wrong. The Dogg can affect what goes on. But this comes at a price. And like William Blake said: 'What is the price of experience? Do men buy it with a song?'

No, it costs you everything.

@ TACK SECURITY

THE BEST FORM OF DEFENCE.

Subject: Destiny Research

We have received notification from our client Dr John Cowie of Destiny Research that you are in possession of certain information connected to the activities of the company.

You should be warned that all information regarding Destiny Research's business activities is proprietary. You are therefore requested to return any such information immediately and without further negotiation. You will not be warned again.

We will know who you are.

Stealth

I haven't had to wait long for the reaction. Cowie's hired a security firm to track me down.

No doubt I'm being tracked down by people I used to hang out with. The underground hacking movement, which started out so free and revolutionary, has now gone corporate.

Their demise has been driven by supply and demand. The Forces of Law and Order didn't have enough computer security experts. The hackers were ahead of them. So the Law changed the rules; they forced the hackers to join up. When we got busted and didn't like the prospect of jail, they'd say, 'Well you don't have to go to prison. There is an alternative. You can work for us. We need your skills.' They made us job offers we couldn't refuse.

So that's how it happened. How a generation of free spirits sold out.

And now they're after me. And they will not take long to find me. Because I'm one of them. I read the same books and loved the same movies. We lived through Sun Tzu and Umberto Eco, Orwell and McLuhan. We danced to Stevie Wonder and Black Sabbath and Lynyrd Skynyrd, Pink Floyd, Acid Jazz, Gregorian Chant, Kraftwerk and The The. We like the same chicks: mostly foreign. Australian, with blue eyes. And we avoided all those vegetarian 'granolas'. We worshipped on the altar of James Brown. And we drank Jose Cuervo till it got light.

Sure they will recognize me. They know the sound of my dreams.

11/05/02   19.20

IT'S FIGHT NIGHT

Table 14: John Cowie

Food	57.50
Drinks	36.80
Gratuity	20.00
Total	113.30

Paid Amex 371176582147722 exp. 06/02

Dr John Cowie File

Call IDS

Cell Data CS

Start	End	number calling	start time
42113	42113	07962482143	19.37
42113	42113	07839443662	22.04

From now on if this guy Cowie moves an inch, the Dogg will know. I have to find something on him, before they find me.

Last night a change in his pattern. He was out visiting a leisure centre in the East End of London. Not the sort of place you'd expect to find a biotech entrepreneur. Suppose he'd say he was out looking for viruses, low life and other bugs.

Picked up this trail when I traced his phone calls to Giselle – I wanted to check he wasn't getting too close to her. One of the calls was made from the East End and when I matched this against his credit card payments it's clear he was at the Sterling Leisure Centre in Leyton for dinner. He paid for two dinners. Not expensive stuff.

First reaction to this info was to think he was meeting a woman; or going for some kind of sexual liaison. Maybe the Sterling Centre was a place he'd pick up a prostitute. So I checked out the place, to see what sort of entertainment went on there. Turns out it hosts all sorts of weird and wonderful acts, from talent contests to boxing. On the night Cowie was there it was holding an unlicensed boxing fight. The place is run by Alan Makin, who checks out as a local fight promoter as well as local pub owner. He deals with Total Martial Arts as well as boxing, so there's some pretty heavy things going down at the Sterling Centre, but Makin is also a born-again Christian. The Dogg wonders what genes he was born with this time!

Anyway, can't tell who Cowie was meeting at the Sterling Centre. But we do know he'll have spent the evening watching two young boys beating the life out of one another, while the crowd is screaming 'Be First. Be First. Be First.' There's usually money involved too; heavy gambling on the outcome. All of which add up to our smart Mr Cowie being involved with some interesting characters, well away from his patch. Sometimes these events can be in aid of local boys' clubs, so maybe Cowie was doing a charity a good turn. But the Dogg is not convinced.

11/05/02

<u>Dr John Cowie File</u>

Match all cc spend with ref. 26924 Leyton

| 10/03/01 | Sterling Leisure Centre | 139.60 |
| 07/07/01 | Sterling Leisure Centre | 255.00 |

corresponding spend previous year

That item on Cowie got me back on his trail. It's from another pattern. Sure enough, it's not the first time Cowie has been to the Sterling Leisure Centre. He went there twice last year; both nights were amateur boxing specials.

So if he's got the violence gene maybe it manifests itself vicariously: he enjoys watching the violence. Could be that's the real truth in what Giselle is finding out – that the gene mutation expresses itself differently in different people: for Gerald it was a straightforward hardman streak, for Stanley it turned in on himself, for Cowie it's vicarious violence and for Shermyn – well we still don't know how it's going to turn out for him. We do know he's been convicted of a crime and that a woman died in the process of him committing that crime. The circumstantial evidence and the character patterns may point another way, but the bare facts remain. Shermyn has killed another human being.

The Dogg has to get a handle on these matters before it's too late.

e-mail to thedogg@acdogg.co.uk

@TACK SECURITY

THE BEST FORM OF DEFENCE.

Subject: Destiny Research

Dogg, we're after your code.

We know where you learned your art.

Get ready to meet your makers.

Stealth

They're trying to frighten the Dogg! Do they really think that bully boy tactics will work on the Dogg?

I am surprised that my contemporaries and former brothers and sisters in the 'inpho' war should resort to the sort of behaviour that just a few years back we'd have associated with the FBI. Reminds me of how mad the FBI got when a bunch of the guys pulled that phone line stunt on them: linked an FBI line to a sex-chat phone line and racked up over $200,000 in fees. The Feds did not enjoy the joke. Their reaction, the words they used, were very similar to Mr Stealth's tone.

Maybe Stealth and I have actually met. When we started out there were only a very few who had the 'Word': how to hack into the global telecommunications network. But that was all a long time ago. He has changed and I have changed. He would say he's doing the right thing, protecting security. I would say that I have seen through that scene. It's about protecting vested interests, not information.

You've got to understand that people are still fighting over who owns the information. Governments, corporations, individuals, all fighting for the right to lock up information – whether it's behind a firewall or a raft of legislation.

But that can't hold any more. It's not a tenable source of power. They should recognize we're all part of the open systems now. You can close the door and lock it and throw away the key, but that ain't much use when you live in a world without walls.

You can't fight the Dogg. He's everywhere, guys. Take me down and I just spring back up in another place and another guise.

You wanna try?

14/05/02   10.14

<u>Dr John Cowie File</u>

<u>Dr John Cowie</u>
Lloyds TSB
Bank Acct   43-16-90   71248623

Withdrawals last 7 days

08/05	cash	£500
10/05	cash	£500
13/05	cash*	£5000

<u>Profile</u>

number of withdrawals of £500 or less in last 6 months =   30

number of withdrawals of >£1000 in last 6 months =   0

*notes to file: phone call 1 from EC2 branch. confirmed status.

What's this, Cowie's on the spend? Drew out five grand in cash. The banks hate giving out cash. Anything over fifty quid and they call out the security guards with their bullet-proof vests to stand by while they're counting it. So for Cowie to take out five grand is a big deal in banking.

If you take in the rest of Cowie's profile I suppose there's not much to be concerned about. I mean it's not as though he can't afford to blow five grand on a night's pleasure. The guy's made a fortune out of biotech companies and the sale of Destiny is going to push him and his colleagues into the seriously rich list. Still that doesn't entirely put the Dogg's mind at rest. A number of scenarios occur to me. First that he's paying someone off, perhaps for past adulteries: maybe the young woman that Social Informatics fingered him with, so to speak, is black-mailing him, threatening to take the story to the press. That would certainly scupper his chances of a knighthood for a while. Or could be that he's spending the money on gambling, waiting for the next of his boxing matches – once you get into that league five grand wouldn't be out of place.

Somehow the Dogg doesn't expect this five grand to just walk away. Not without burning a hole in his pocket.

Dr John Cowie File

0774332941

Log calls to 01632 960007/0777684329

Date	Number called	Time	Duration
13/05/02	0777684329	10.05	06.31

Call IDS

Cell Data (A)

Date	Start	End	Number	Start time
13/05/02	46217	46217	0777684329	12.03
13/05/02	44693	44693	0777684329	15.21

The phone calls keep coming. Cowie must be getting pretty desperate, calling Giselle from all over.

He's in East London again but this time he's there at lunch time not in the evening. I check out the credit card items. Nothing. Then I focus in on the geo-co-ordinates of his telephone call.

I recognize the numbers. The call was made from the St George and Dragon pub in Stratford High Street. The same pub where Gerald had his fight. Why would Cowie be in a pub that's known for illegal fighting, and is the favourite drinking hole of some very unsavoury characters?

I do some more digging. The St George is owned by a Mr Alan Makin, the boxing promoter and owner of the Sterling Leisure Centre. The manager of the St George is a Mr Seamus O'Hanlon – an ex-fighter. Suddenly the connection with the fight game makes sense: where better to get data on violence than the boxing game? There's blood on the canvas every day. Cowie's doing his own research. He has been for a while. I'd bet ever since he read Giselle's original paper – the one he got cancelled. It fascinated Cowie. The violence gene. That would be something worth patenting.

Now we know why he's so sure of Giselle's results – he's proved them for himself. And while he was watching the boxing, he got a taste for it.

The five grand that Cowie has withdrawn is probably to pay off a debt within this circle, perhaps for blood samples from the ring.

14/05/02   15.16

Subject: Test Results

Dear Ms Jackson

We have matched the results from sample 18342432 against the genetic data you have supplied and can now confirm a correlation. As you requested we have also carried out a proteomic SMI on the sample and have detected conspicuous levels of D2DR. Full report attached.

Kind regards

Kim Bolton

www.esainc.com/MolecularProteomics/molecular_proteomics.htm

DNA is just predisposition. Protein is function.

_____

Proteomics is vastly expanding our knowledge of cellular and tissue function.

There is information contained within the cell or tissue that represents the cumulative effects of all expressed and modified proteins. This information is stored in the small molecular inventory (SMI) of the cell. The SMI is a pattern of molecules that reflects the cell's status.

The mining of this data is Molecular Proteomics™. It is the interface between proteomics and chemical biology.

While the genome is representative of what might be, the proteome is what is expressed.

The SMI gives a direct picture of the proteome activity and its environment. It presents a powerful portrait, reflecting health, disease, aging and the effects of drugs and the environment.

Watching over Giselle, reading everything that comes into her account – before she does. She's got the information she was looking for: Shermyn has tested positive again.

Once might have been a mistake, twice and it's no coincidence.

Giselle also ran a proteomic test on Shermyn's sample. Did some scurrying around on this and as far as the Dogg can make out it's a test of proteins in the blood. Gives you another way into the genetic data. It tells you what's happening right now. Like the guys say, DNA is predisposition. But proteomics is function. In other words, with proteomics Giselle can tell whether or not the violence gene is turned on inside Shermyn. And guess what? It is. The boy's so tight he's ready to snap.

Subject: Your Tests

Dear Shermyn

I have had the tests back from the lab and would like to arrange to meet. We need to talk them through. Unfortunately, I am rather busy tying up the loose ends of a project I have been working on and wonder whether we could meet in Oxford instead of London. I would be happy to reimburse your costs. Would Tuesday 21st May, late afternoon/early evening be all right for you?

e-mail from shermynf@innocenti.co.uk

Subject: Re: Your Tests

Dear Ms Jackson

Thank you for your email (I note your new address) and the offer of a meeting. I can drive to Oxford. Maybe we could meet in the centre somewhere around 7 pm?

best

Shermyn Frazier

This is going too far, taking too many risks. Giselle is acting the typical scientist with a conscience. She thinks it's the responsible thing to do to break the news to Shermyn personally. She's wrong. The scientist is not responsible for the result, and does not need to meet the subject of the experiment. The mouse in the cage will not thank her for it.

Shermyn has tested positive. He's not going to be able to handle the bad news. The only thing that's kept him going is the hope of innocence. His inner story. If he has that taken away from him, if he discovers that no matter what he believes about himself the truth is different, there will be nothing left to hold him together. And I for one wouldn't want to be around when that happens.

I send her a note, asking her not to get drawn in. She's taking risks with Cowie and his company lawyers, but they're professional risks. They get sorted out over the solicitor's desk. This stuff with Shermyn is infinitely more unpredictable, because it involves an individual whose life is on the line.

Dear Dogg

Thanks for your concern. I can handle myself. Besides 'You never walk alone'.

G

www.wired.com/news/medtech/0,1286,42317,00.html

When football fans learned that their faces were scanned and compared to the mugshots of common criminals at this year's Superbowl, many were outraged.

The facial scans work by converting images into numerical codes that can be easily stored and searched in large databases.

It all started with the <u>FERET program</u>, a Department of Defense initiative in the early 1990s to determine the viability of using algorithms to measure faces.

Application for facial recognition technology falls into two categories: identification and surveillance.

The Dogg thought that this would be the reaction. Defiant but still with a plan.

Giselle is driven by conscience. She still wants to make the world a better place, and of course that can only be done alone.

But then there's the come-on, the element that gets Dogg every time: 'You never walk alone.' Knowing just how to get involved. Not by a request but a little taunt.

And sure enough the Dogg cannot let her go unprotected. I look at the picture downloaded from the Destiny site. It provokes a connection: the photo was taken for a building's image recognition system. So why not use it for that purpose but on a wider system? It's already being done – at a football match or shopping mall near you. All you need is the facial recognition software and you can start automatically matching faces against any set of televisual images; on any CCTV system, anywhere.

Feed in the image and the Dogg will be able to watch over her wherever she goes. Too right. 'You never walk alone.'

LINK TO CCTV SYSTEM

Match

IP add 65.104.93.35
WAN 1267/43
Time 18.45 21.05.02
B/W 510(H) x 492(H)
3.2 fps

www.oxford.gov.uk

CCTV BOOST

released 05/03/2001

NEW cameras are planned to extend Oxford's successful city centre CCTV security system. The City Council launched a funding bid for three new areas: Worcester Street South/Park End Street, Friars Entry and the area around St Ebbe's. Meanwhile recent figures showed there were 465 arrests directly due to CCTV in the system's first 18 months. The log book also records a number of cases of CCTV staff working together with the operators of the Oxford University security camera system and with city centre retailers using the Radiolink messaging link.

www.brookes.ac.uk/schools/social/law

RECENT PAPERS AND PUBLICATIONS ON CCTV

Report on the 1999 Oxford City Centre Fear of Crime Surveys 2000
Fear of Crime and attitudes to CCTV in Oxford City Centre
CCTV and Human Rights, CCTV special SixTV

www.cctvconsult.com

IP, Internet Protocol, Address works as a website address on the Internet. When it is assigned to a Web Camera, you can open its video page with any web browser such as Microsoft Internet Explorer or Netscape by typing in the IP numbers.

The facial recognition software is working. I can see Giselle. She's in Oxford, on the move. She's wearing an overcoat and scarf. Trousers, calf-length boots and shoulder bag. She is walking briskly.

She is going down St Giles, past St John's College, up to the corner and the Ashmolean Museum. She waits at the corner. The lights turn and the traffic stops.

Switch camera.

She crosses Beaumont Street, past the Randolph Hotel and on towards Broad Street. Now she's in a pedestrian zone, Cornmarket. It's getting late – there are few shoppers left. A guy from the *Big Issue* offers her a magazine, she shakes her head, smiles and turns into Burger King.

Switch camera.

LINK TO CCTV SYSTEM

Match

IP add 67.103.92.41
LAN 643/L2
Time 18.51 21.05.02
B/W 510(H) x 492(H)
3.2 fps
Quadscreen

www.cctvconsult.com

Public IP address is for the Internet like a public phone number that you can call from any phones connected to the telephone service. Private IP Address, like an intercom number inside an organization, works only within a limited area such as a LAN or WAN system.

Giselle walks in through Burger King doors. Four-way split screen picture. One screen is on the entrance, another at the counter and a young black guy who is frying a burger pattie. Another screen watches the back door to the site, with dustbins and empty cartons in shot; another screen picks out three young white girls seated at a table.

Giselle walks forward. Out of shot.

Pick her up at the counter. She orders a drink. Coke. She turns, looks for a seat. Goes over to the table next to the three white girls. One of the girls takes a bite of her burger. Ketchup leaks from the side and falls on the table, she wipes it with a paper napkin.

Giselle settles with her back to the wall. Bag on her lap, reaches in and takes out her mobile phone. Checks the readout – maybe she's checking for calls – and then puts it back in the bag. She stares at the entrance, waiting for an arrival.

A young black male walks in. She looks up at him. He avoids her stare and moves out of shot.

The three girls get up and walk out. As they reach the doorway another young black male walks in. He lets them pass. He looks around. Walks out of frame.

Young black male standing at the counter, looks around. Only lone female is Giselle. He walks over to her. She stands. She holds out her hand and they shake. She speaks smiling. He returns the smile. This is Shermyn.

The guy at the counter flips over a burger pattie. At the back entry wind blows a cellophane wrapper off an empty carton and down the alleyway.

Shermyn is wearing short bomber jacket and jeans, trainers. Also carrying a sports bag. He's medium build, with glasses. They talk for a few moments. She motions towards her drink, he shakes his head. Body language suggests he wants to leave. She nods, takes drink from cup. Replaces cup on the table, and walks to door. Shermyn follows her.

The guy at the counter flips another pattie.

LINK TO CCTV SYSTEM

Match

IP add 73.112.42.95
WAN 1267521
Time 19.16 21.05.02
B/W 510(H) x 492(H)
3.2 fps

Pick up Giselle and Shermyn at the corner of St Aldates and the High Street. They walk on past the covered market. They're in conversation.

They reach the University of Oxford shop. They stop, she turns to him, talking direct to him.

The Dogg is shouting at the screen: 'OK, Giselle, tell him quick. Tell him he's tested positive. Give him the data and get out of this scene.'

Shermyn's head drops forward. Almost involuntary movement. Giselle's still talking to him.

He's shaking his head. They start walking again. He's shaking his head more agitatedly, mouthing 'No, no.'

She's at his side. Reaches into her bag. Takes out a CD, holds it up towards him.

And the Dogg is yelling: 'That's it, Giselle, tell him the data doesn't lie. Tell him it's the truth, then get out of there. You've satisfied your moral imperatives. Go now.'

Walking along past University College towards the Examination Schools. She's still got the CD in her hand, he brushes it away. She puts the CD back in her bag. As she does so he grabs her arm. Drags her towards him, right, into an alley at the Examination Schools.

They go out of shot.

LINK TO CCTV SYSTEM

No match

IP add	73.112.42.31	19.21
IP add	64.103.65.98	19.22
IP add	45.210.38.49	19.22
IP add	15.132.65.94	19.22

www.cctvconsult.com

Another excellent feature of the web camera is that you can program it to send you an e-mail with up to 5 pictures when a movement is detected by the camera. And it usually has enough flash memory for you to customize your own Internet home page.

The Dogg is screaming. Screaming at the picture, 'Come back into the picture, Giselle, walk back into the frame.

'Tell me it's all right.

'I want to see your image back again.'

The High Street is empty. Cut to camera outside Magdalen College. A few students on bikes travel through frame.

Cut to camera in Longwall Street. Traffic passing through shot. No pedestrians.

Cut to camera along Rose Lane. Empty.

The Dogg is screaming at the cameras, 'Come back into shot, Giselle. Walk back in.'

21/05/02   19.25

IP add 21.103.65.94 19.25
IP add 23.156.54.63 19.25
IP add 54.101.35.36 19.25
IP add 52.148.35.64 19.25
IP add 24.154.23.89 19.25
IP add 42.114.52.97 19.25
IP add 45.114.25.75 19.25
IP add 12.210.35.64 19.25
IP add 65.242.35.54 19.25
IP add 84.231.56.25 19.25
IP add 33.120.65.32 19.25
IP add 14.125.32.65 19.25
IP add 52.105.32.55 19.25
IP add 52.105.32.51 19.25
IP add 11.102.65.54 19.25
IP add 06.111.32.54 19.25
IP add 94.112.31.24 19.25
IP add 16.132.01.05 19.25

No match

Mobile phone monitor
0777684329
no calls

Have been searching through all of the city cameras for the last hour and a half. There is no sign of Giselle. Fleeting likenesses in other passers-by, but no Giselle. Her algorithm doesn't match with anything on screen.

She's off the radar. She must have gone home another way. Taken a bus or something from the other side of town or stopped off to see some friends. Yeah, she's bound to have friends all over Oxford. That's it, she's out having dinner with friends.

No need to use her mobile phone, they were expecting her. She'll turn up in a little while. No worries, Dogg.

Even so, I wish Giselle would come back to the screen, or make a call, or just arrive back home. It's been long enough now.

Police National Crime Files
CAD (Computer Aided Dispatch) Report

RECORDED IN IR BY CC00875 AT 20:09 SERIAL 10187

REC BY: CCC:IR
PHONE: 01632 960004
LOCATION: O\S PORT MEADOW   28:185029
TYPE: 53\SUS   SECTOR: GD
GRADE: I
CALLER: MR SMITH
VRM:
CLASS:
ASSIGN: G2, GD1, GM81, TJ421, GD1

SS\T21\231-5
OCCUPIER OF NO. 34 ACOL STREET MAY BE AT RISK OF DOMESTIC
VIOLENCE. SEE SPECIAL SCHEMES TOPIC 21 PAGE 231-235

TIME	USER ID	REMARKS
20:09:04	17785677	^ INFT STATES HE HAS FOUND A BODY OF FEMALE A\A 35YRS AT LOCN. BLVD GUNSHOT WOUND. NFDS
20:09:10	17785677	H.A.T.S. TEAM INFORMED. LOCAL UNIT TO ATTEND PLSE.
20:10:01	CC0218	SI ^ GD PLSE CAN WE HAVE TRIDENT CONTACT TEL.

I'm with the police in real time, linked into the computer dispatch reports that work alongside emergency calls. There's been an incident in Oxford. Grade I for immediate response.

A body has been found in the Port Meadow area. Female. Aged about 35. Shot.

They've called in HATS, the homicide team, as well as Trident, the gun crimes unit. CC0218 is the signal for Scotland Yard.

If HATS have been called we would suspect the woman is dead, but the report says NFDS. No further details, so the death is unconfirmed.

Interesting how the language and code take any feeling out of the situation. Doing what they're supposed to do: translating life into data. Me, I'm translating data back into life, explaining the codes so that I feel closer to the incident.

But that's not going to help. The thing we have to cling to is the facts. Port Meadow is quite a long way from where we last saw Giselle. It's unlikely that the two incidents are related.

And in the back of my mind I hear the call. 'Let it be a false positive. Don't let it be Giselle.'

Police National Crime Files
CAD (Computer Aided Dispatch) Report

RECORDED IN UH BY CL00961 AT 20:16 SERIAL: 26421

REC BY: JPL:UH
PHONE
LOCATION: HEADINGTON ROAD
TYPE: 42/RTA
GRADE: 1
ASSIGN: F2, GF82, F56, WV7

TIME	USER ID	REMARKS
20:16:47	26264133	SPD CHECK, STLN CAR PURSUIT GS8, NOT STOPPING ASSIST PLSE
20:19:39	26264133	RTA, CRASH, PEDN HURT SHOP DAMAGE, DRIVER IC3 RUNNING, URGENT ASSIST PLSE GL7932 IN PURSUIT AERIAL ASSIST PLSE

LINK TO CCTV SYSTEM

IP add 72.102.43.12   20:22   21.05.02

Searching . . .

Still nothing more of the woman found on Port Meadow. An ambulance has taken the body to the John Radcliffe. It's still en route now. Waiting for it to arrive so I can pick it up on external CCTV.

Meanwhile the CAD wires are lighting up with another incident. A police chase. Routine patrol spotted a car driving at speed. Checked the number plates, identified the vehicle as stolen and began pursuit. The stolen vehicle refused to stop. After a brief chase the driver of the vehicle lost control and crashed into a corner shop in the Headington area. One pedestrian has been hurt. The driver, a young black male, fled the scene on foot and police are still in pursuit.

Shermyn?

The ambulance from Port Meadow has arrived back at the John Radcliffe. A stretcher is taken out of the rear doors. Can't make out the identity of the body on the stretcher. It all happens so quick and then they're inside the hospital.

21/05/02   23.28

<u>**Dr Giselle Jackson File**</u>

John Radcliffe Hospital
Coroner's Report
<u>GISELLE FRANCINE JACKSON</u>

one emerald ring on third finger of right hand
TAG Heuer watch on left arm
silver bangle bracelet on left arm
gold/garnet bracelet on left arm
pearl necklace
cream blouse
pink cotton trousers
black boots
tattoo of rose on right breast
bruising to right wrist and forearm
gunshot wound in head, centre front of left ear, exiting about 2" above right
ear

Pronounced dead at 21.07

Death is the wrong data. It's empty and silent and although the file doesn't close it does grow cold. The life withers. The interaction ceases. And you are less, Dogg.

Yet this is your responsibility. You broke the rule. You crossed over. You told her things she had not asked to know. All events have followed on from that. You're paying the price of experience.

If you influence the action, you must be there at the curtain call. Tonight they will not be throwing flowers. And you will be the only one shouting 'Encore. Giselle. Encore. Like you're walking on air.'

Everyone else is quiet, Dogg. Just looking at you. They've turned round to look at the guy who's sitting in the production booth above the auditorium. The guy with the headphones on, his hands at the controls. This is the guy who's not supposed to be seen. Who's only noticed when something goes wrong: when the lights don't come up when they should do, or the curtains get stuck. You're not allowed to be part of the action. Strictly production.

So get the show back up.

It's a murder mystery, remember.

The victim was shot dead. Point blank. Nasty, pre-planned, not heat of the moment stuff.

Take it from here.

e-mail to thedogg@acdogg.co.uk

@TACK SECURITY

THE BEST FORM OF DEFENCE.

Subject: Destiny Research

Dogg, we've got the code.

Say goodbye to your loved ones.

Remember Morris.

Stealth

More from Stealth at @tack Security. Don't get the feeling he's going to give up. He has a contract on me. And that's not all. His note has a code word in it. 'Morris'. Stands for Robert Morris, the guy from Cornell University who invented the first computer worm back in 1988. As we know, the worm went mad, replicating and infecting machines everywhere. To professionals like me in the online community, 'Morris' means this threat is for real. A virus will be coming my way.

Yesterday I wouldn't have been so worried. But yesterday Giselle was still alive. She was breathing. Now she's not. She's been murdered by some fanatic with a violence gene. And who's to say Stealth isn't suffering from the same mutation?

I have stepped out into the real world and the world is getting back at me. I myself am in the firing line. And while I'm thinking about Giselle I'm more vulnerable than ever. The only thing that will keep me 'alive' is finding some raw piece of data to defend myself with. And that takes time and a clear mind.

24/05/02

Police National Crime Files
CAD (Computer Aided Dispatch) Report

RECORDED IN IR BY CC00875 AT 09:14 SERIAL 10187

SUSP ARRESTED.

The police have acted fast, real fast. They've pinned the murder on Shermyn quicker than the Dogg could have hoped.

But then I suppose that's it, you are guilty, Shermyn. You were born to be guilty. And you know what, the irony is that it's your past record that's really going to do you in this time: a stolen car, a woman killed. You'll plead innocent, same broken record, Shermyn.

And this time, Shermyn, the technology's caught up with you. You're on the CCTV, pushing her around. So there's going to be no defence for this action. No matter what you tell them about Project Iago.

Maybe Giselle wanted this to happen. She wanted to prove herself right. And of course, in that moment Shermyn would also be her insurance policy. As if she were saying: 'If anything happens to me while delivering news of genetic tests to Shermyn Frazier, please put all the media attention on Destiny Research, my former employer. They have all the details of the experiment I was heading up. Details that my former employer wishes to keep secret, but which the public must know about.'

Yeah that's it, girl, you knew what you were doing. It was a win/win situation. You thought that if you pushed Shermyn hard enough, he'd break. But you'd still get what you wanted: publicity for your discovery. Everyone would know about your gene.

Police National Crime Files

CAD 26421 refers PC GL07932 EDWARDS takes report at GL STN OFFICE

SUSP1, a male IC3, A/A 25, was identified as driving a stolen vehicle at speed, and refused to stop. Police gave chase and vehicle subsequently crashed into shop AS LITTLE on Headington Road. SUSP1 fled the scene, GL7932 in pursuit. SUSP1 was observed throwing a package into a garden, later identified as a handgun (Rep 114523 refers).
SUSP1 was apprehended and brought to station for questioning. SUSP1 identified as Grant WILLIAMS (previous record 3824/C refers). On further questioning WILLIAMS made no reply.
Retrieved handgun matches with gun wound to head Giselle JACKSON (CAD 10187 refers) and DNA forensic report matches blood on WILLIAMS jacket to victim.

Vehicle searched (Rep 156234 refers), black leather handbag found.

On further questioning WILLIAMS denied any knowledge of JACKSON or the handgun.

WILLIAMS was charged by GL 7932 with vehicle theft, damage by dangerous driving and murder. He made no comment.

REPORT 156234

1 Black leather handbag, contents

1 purse – containing credit cards, cash, driving licence
Identity DR GISELLE JACKSON
1 mobile phone
1 leather diary
1 CD computer disk – Destiny Research
1 African carved figure
1 set keys
1 car key
1 packet tissues
1 letter – invoice Wigmore St Clinic/Shermyn Frazier
1 packet paracetamol

It wasn't Shermyn.

The man driving the stolen vehicle did a runner across some open fields. The police gave chase and he was seen throwing an item into a back garden as he ran. The police put up a helicopter and brought in more muscle and eventually caught up with the guy on a set of allotments south of Headington. He was a young black guy all right, but not Shermyn. And the item he threw into someone's garden was a pistol.

The police took him back to the station and started questioning him about the gun and what he was doing with it. The young black guy turns out to be a Mr Grant Williams. Unsavoury character, known to work as a minder and fixer for London criminals. Forensics matched the gun he threw away with the weapon used to shoot Giselle and it's a perfect fit. DNA of a fleck of blood on Grant Williams' jacket matched Giselle's: the possibility of error was 1 in several million. And the police also recovered Giselle's shoulder bag inside the stolen vehicle. No doubt about it. This was the guy who had shot Giselle. Single shot to the head. From close up. It was a professional hit.

Of course, Williams wasn't saying anything at this stage. In fact he was still claiming his innocence. But they didn't buy that. Williams was known as a fixer for the London mob. This was a contract hit. No other explanation was possible. The police concluded that robbery was an unlikely motive as the only item stolen was Giselle's shoulder bag containing a few credit cards and a CD with Destiny Research marked on it. Mr Williams had no known connection with Giselle so there was little evidence that this was the work of some possessed stalker.

None of it made much sense, except if you knew the sort of men that Giselle had been mixing with over the last few months. Dangerous men, men with bad genes.

<u>Dr Giselle Jackson File</u>

OXFORDSHIRE POLICE

Case No.   13399

Status   Murder Enquiry

Victim   Dr Giselle Jackson

Ongoing

Suspect MR GRANT WILLIAMS' eighth interview since incident. Suspect now wishes to make statement as to the background to the incident. Confirms that he shot the deceased with single shot from handgun owned by himself. He claims that he was hired to carry out shooting by the manager of the St George public house in Stratford High Street, London E10. He also claims he was paid £5000 for the job.

Subsequent interview with manager of St George public house, MR SEAMUS O'HANLON. MR O'HANLON denies any knowledge of DR GISELLE JACKSON. Calls the accusations 'laughable'. Claims he has no knowledge of anyone called DR GISELLE JACKSON. Investigating officers can establish no link between the deceased and MR O'HANLON.

Reading the notes you can see why the police are mystified. Why should an eminent genetic scientist get shot in Oxford by a black bloke who's never met her before and yet who claims he was hired by the manager of a pub in London, who also has no apparent connection with Giselle?

It doesn't make sense because there's one missing piece in the puzzle: Dr John Cowie.

Now we know why Cowie went to the St George pub. He was there to hire a professional. He needed to go through an intermediary to break the chain of association. And he needed that intermediary to be so far from Giselle's world that the link between himself and Giselle would be almost impossible to make. You have to hand it to him. It was a smart move.

If the hitman makes a clean job and gets away with it – he gets his five grand and walks free. If he gets caught, there's nothing to link him to Cowie and without that link how are the police going to make any charge on the pub manager who acted as the go-between? Because for the police it comes back to the question: why should a publican in London want a leading Oxford research scientist dead? No reason, so the publican walks free.

I guess there's a certain justice in that: the hitman shouldn't have got caught. The fact that he was caught out by chance, by the fluke that a police car saw him driving fast, checked the number plates and then went in pursuit of a stolen car – well that's for God to work out, not me.

Can I prove anything against Cowie? No. Just because he was in the St George pub for an hour or so doesn't mean he's guilty of Giselle's murder. Unless you know he is.

I have just looked back at the CCTV footage of Giselle in Oxford. She goes into the Burger King. A few moments later a young black male walks in. She looks up at him. He avoids her stare. That young black male was Grant Williams.

Dr Giselle Jackson File

OXFORDSHIRE POLICE

Case No.   13399

Date   27/05/02   Time: 15.30

Status   Murder Enquiry

Victim   Dr Giselle Jackson

Ongoing

<u>Interview Shermyn Frazier</u>

Mr FRAZIER agreed to come forward for interview even though he is not a suspect in this case. Mr FRAZIER confirmed that he was with the deceased Ms GISELLE JACKSON on the evening of her death. He agreed to meet her in Oxford to discuss the results of a recent blood test. Mr FRAZIER discussed these results while walking with Dr JACKSON through central Oxford (CCTV coverage confirms this). Their discussion became agitated at one point as Dr JACKSON informed Mr FRAZIER that in her opinion the results of the blood tests proved that Mr SHERMYN FRAZIER carried a gene which in her opinion could result in violent behaviour. Ms JACKSON claimed that the proof of this was contained on a CD in her possession at that time. This CD has since been returned to its owners Destiny Research. Mr FRAZIER confirmed that he argued with Ms JACKSON over the implications of these results and left her when they were unable to reach an agreement as to what he should do next. Mr FRAZIER left Ms JACKSON at approximately 7.40 p.m. and returned to his car. He called his brother on his mobile phone when he reached his car. The call has been traced and confirmed.

In my concern for Giselle, I have overlooked the implication of that evening meeting in Oxford for Shermyn. I don't think he's in danger from Cowie – after all, who would believe an ex-con if he comes along with some story about the violence gene – but he may be in danger from himself.

What is Shermyn going to do with his new knowledge? What do you do with self-knowledge that goes beyond your own skin? It's one thing to keep things a secret which only concern yourself, quite another when that secret has implications for others. What about Jason? The big brother who's supported Shermyn through thick and thin. Doesn't he deserve to know about the tests and that Shermyn proved positive?

Shermyn can't just deny the data. He can't say that's not me. He has a responsibility to Jason and his immediate family and to his future wife and his future children and maybe even to the whole of society, to let them know. Or does he? In his opinion the secret is safest with him. He may not feel impelled to tell others. What's more, they may not want to know.

29/05/02   13.41

<u>**Shermyn Frazier File**</u>

<u>www.wereallinnocentvictims.com</u>

VOICES FROM FORGOTTEN VICTIMS – DEDICATED TO INNOCENT FAMILY MEMBERS OF PRISON INMATES

The purpose of this page is to provide a gathering place for all the forgotten victims to share their experiences, fears, hopes and dreams with others in the same situation. It is also my hope that those visitors who have never had a loved one in prison will leave with a new perspective of what it really feels like to 'Do Time With a Loved One'. You may even leave with a new friend.

You are listening to 'It Matters to Me' by Faith Hill – BECAUSE MY BROTHER SHERMYN MATTERS A GREAT DEAL TO ME and YOU MATTER TO ME.

Please take a moment to visit some of the websites in the 'Families Doing Time Together' webring. If you are a family member of a prisoner, and you have a website, please consider joining today.

WE ARE FAMILY. WHEN ONE SUFFERS WE ALL SUFFER.

<u>Shermyn is innocent</u>

click here if you want to help Shermyn Frazier – with information, support or just your love.

<u>Update</u> . . .

'We're going back to court'

The news we've been waiting for. Car thief Paul Garsden has confirmed that he took part in an incident involving the theft of a red Peugeot in the Hackney area the night that Shermyn was found behind the wheel of the crashed vehicle. That's what we've been waiting for, the first crack in the story. It proves Shermyn was telling the truth. We're going back to court. It will be a long struggle, brothers, but we will prove Shermyn's innocence. We will prove that this was a racist conviction on the part of the police and the whole judicial system. They are the guilty ones, not Shermyn.

We know what Shermyn's decision is. He is going to deny the data. Turn his back on the blood data. He will not allow anything to come in the way of his pursuit of innocence.

The Dogg must hand it to him. That's perseverance. And the Dogg must also say on the facts, Shermyn is indeed probably innocent. He may have the gene, but it hasn't turned to violence. Perhaps there are flaws in Giselle's project.

Of course she'd say 'It's only a matter of time.' He is guilty, he just won't accept it. All we need to wait for is the right trigger. That's why it's wrong to deny the data, Shermyn. You have to go with it; live with it. Because others will know about you. Sooner or later the truth will out and the truth will ask us to go beyond these borders and arrive in a new place and find new laws for life.

The Dogg, for one, will take time to find a place in this new territory. The data that Giselle has left me with will change everything about my work. I have a new way of detection. I can know the guilty before the crime. I have Giselle to thank for that. But I was not there to help her.

Dr Giselle Jackson File

OXFORDSHIRE POLICE

Case No.   13399

Date   30/05/02   Time: 10.30

Status   Murder Enquiry

Victim   Dr Giselle Jackson

Ongoing

Interview Dr John Cowie
CEO Destiny Research

Dr COWIE agreed to be interviewed in order to help police in their investigations and in particular to endeavour to establish a motive for the attack on Ms JACKSON. Mr COWIE informed police that Dr JACKSON had recently left the employ of Destiny Research. The company was exploring links with an American business and given that much of Destiny's research work might be transferred to the US, Dr JACKSON had decided she would rather pursue her career in Britain than abroad. Dr COWIE had been saddened by Dr JACKSON's decision and had on numerous occasions endeavoured to get her to reconsider. He was mystified by the murder of Dr JACKSON and although she was engaged in sensitive genetic studies for the company, Dr COWIE could not see any link between her murder and her work as a scientist. The company was setting up a fund in her name to pursue genetic testing in areas such as heart disease and lung cancer.

Dr COWIE denied that Mr SHERMYN FRAZIER had been among those who had agreed to participate in Destiny's own research programmes. Any relationship between Mr FRAZIER and Dr JACKSON must have occurred outside of Dr JACKSON's work at Destiny Research.

Cowie goes into the police interview as bold as you like. They've got nothing on him, there's nothing to worry about. In fact he's got a lot to thank the police for. They returned the CD with Giselle's files on it, the Project Iago files. Couldn't have turned out better for him.

Giselle was never going to stop this from happening. Even if she'd been right about the way Shermyn would react. Even if she'd triggered the violence inside him, in the Dogg's opinion that was never going to be enough. She needed more support, more money and more genetic data than she could ever hope to assemble working on her own. She was out of her depth. She didn't need to die for Cowie to get what he wanted. That's where the balance goes wrong. That's where the evil slides in.

All the while Cowie thinks he's getting away with it.

But there is of course one surprise waiting for him. Or maybe I should say one test of his character. When he opens the Project Iago files on the CD and goes to the Control Group data, he'll have the choice as to whether to leave his name in the 'tested positive' column or not. If he acts as I expect him to, he will delete his name and that logic-bomb which I planted on the files during my hack will kick into action. I'd love to be there to watch, as Cowie sees the whole of his research disappear. And all because of a simple choice: if he had been willing to share the data with others, the file would have survived. But because he wants to own and keep the data for himself, the whole thing will delete and purge. Right before his eyes.

@TACK SECURITY

THE BEST FORM OF DEFENCE.

Subject: Destiny Research

Dogg

We have invented a new virus. We have named it after you. Because it will destroy you and only you. It will come across the net one day . . .

Think of it as a soulmate, Dogg. It's the only one you're going to have.

Stealth

There's no doubting this Stealth's persistence. He's going to get the contract done on me whatever it takes. And it would appear that he has designed a particularly unpleasant end for Dogg. A personalized virus. One that will come across the globe and search the Dogg out wherever he lies. Reactive only to the Dogg's DNA. Coded to him.

Hardly the noble art of warfare, but effective.

The Dogg reckons he has only one move to make.

I came away from that hack of the Destiny Research system with two things. First, that picture of Giselle. It was something that I wished to protect. Funny how it's worked out.

But the Dogg has now realized it is the only thing that can protect him.

I have sent this picture to John Cowie. As a keepsake, you could say. I mentioned in my note to him that I would send this picture along with the whole of my 'Dr Giselle Jackson' file, including mobile phone logs, to his son Master William Cowie. I would suggest that if his son wished to know any more about Dr Jackson, he could ask his mother, who would no doubt recognize Dr Jackson from the picture taken by Social Informatics some eight years ago.

I said to Dr Cowie that he was presented with a choice: he could accept that his son would know all about the circumstances of Dr Jackson's death and the genetic information derived from Project Iago, or he could let the whole matter against me drop. Blackmail is not noble, I admit, but at least I would survive.

And there are some things you just don't want to keep in the family.

@TACK SECURITY

THE BEST FORM OF DEFENCE.

Subject: Destiny Research

Dogg

The contract on you has been withdrawn. But don't forget you now have a virus named after you. Morris is waiting . . .

Stealth

Proves Dogg's theory: if you're in a shoot-out, fire second. That way you're either dead or you'll know the other guy has missed.

Stealth has slid back into his lair and although he does so with a snarl, the parting threat leaves the Dogg unimpressed.

Do I need more revenge? Possibly, but if I'm any judge of character I know that I've hurt him. I can tell that he watched as his precious research file was deleted and purged right before his eyes. He's lost the chance to patent the 'Iago' gene and so his deal with North West Industries will fall through. It won't hold him back for long, but I suspect it's a better result than we could have bargained by other means.

He will also feel uncomfortable that he has had to leave a problem unresolved: the Dogg. I could be back to bother him at any time. It would not be in my best interests, but still it is a worry for him. And his family.

But the final and best revenge lies inside him. Dr Cowie is discovering his true potential, his potential for self-sabotage. He knows – and cannot unknow – that he is carrying the violence gene inside him. Tick, tock. Waiting to go off.

PROJECT IAGO

Variation 1186

cagtgagccg agatcgcgcc actgcactcc   agtctgtgtg acagagtgac agcccgtctc

And you? I have bought you time. Nothing more. The work on Project Iago will begin again. Cowie has already done the groundwork.

In the meantime, here's the second item I brought back from my hack into Destiny Research. The genetic code at the heart of Project Iago. Do you recognize it? Maybe not. You probably don't have the violence gene. But I thought I should give you the code just in case. You might want to check yourself out. You see, from now on you have to view yourself differently.

Prick yourself and you don't bleed, you download. Your veins are full of data, genetic code. Like any data it can be stored, retrieved and mined. People in labs all over the world are gaining access to it. They're searching for patterns. In silico. Testing your data against the current knowledge.

So although you may test negative today, that's not going to help you. With thousands of new genetic patents being registered every year, it's just a matter of time. Until they find something on you.

Your crime isn't on record yet, that's all. But one day it will be. And you won't be the first to know.

If you want to hire me, you know where I am.

ACKNOWLEDGEMENTS

The Dogg may work alone, but he is not so foolish or proud as to claim this book is all his own doing. He would like to thank Nikolas Rose, Professor John Bell, Jenny Taylor and Dr Justin Turner for their invaluable expert advice.

Sarah Hoffbrand, Farhat Zaheer, Celia Lury, Richard Fryer, Ian Karet, David Womersley, Karen Lury, Tom Squire and Jo Sadler all made telling contributions to the case.

To the Dogg's mentor, Bill Scott-Kerr, for his unswerving support and many good ideas, respect. To all the team at Transworld who kept the investigation on track and to Julian Alexander for teaching the Dogg many new tricks, salud. And to Laura Wolverson for making sure the world knows where the Dogg is at, many thanks.

Finally the Dogg would like to pay special tribute to Claire and Lyndall. Only they know how much the Dogg owes them.

DANGEROUS DATA
by lury.gibson

HOW MUCH DO YOU WANT TO KNOW?

Every move you take, every payment you make, creates data. Personal data about you. Facts that exist in a timeless present, because nothing can ever be truly erased.

Maybe it seems like individually, facts don't matter. It's just a set of unrelated data, right? Dream on. Someone's looking through it. Sifting. Data mining. Discovering your secrets.

Someone like Dogg. Data Detective. The best there is . Give him some-one's name and he'll sell you a life story. That's what happens. With one little fact, Dogg can unravel a hidden world. What appears to start as an innocent investigation becomes an intimate intrigue of drugs, sex and suspicious deaths.

All Dogg had to do was start looking. You could be his next client – or his next victim. That indiscreet little office e-mail you penned last week – you think it has disappeared? Not a chance.

Welcome to the end of privacy.

'A new breed of thriller . . . terrifyingly convincing . . . I doubt there will be a more important book published this year' *Guardian*

'A compelling, gripping thriller with a highly successful gimmick' *The Big Issue*

'A remote control love story with a sting in the tail . . . A clever little classic' *The Times*

'Frighteningly good . . . terrifying, not least because much of it is believable' *Arena*

'Compelling reading for conspiracy theorists who might realise that this Dogg's bark is all about bytes' *i-D*

0 552 14870 9